BY JAMES DALBY

Moscow Assassin

By

JAMES
DALBY

This book is Fiction

All characters in this book are fictitious **except** for President of Russia and the names of Russians who have been assassinated.

The place names are correct as is the equipment in the story.

***

The story about St. Lucia Airways being owned and run by the CIA is true. The author was aware of the incident.

***

The fact that the CIA has a place in Florida for the families of deceased agents is also true. A friend of ours was taken there with her children after her husband was killed in Angola.

***

The story of people being flown strapped to the outside of an Apache helicopter is factual.

***

The percentage of Russians living in parts of Lithuania is factual.

***

The method of controlling cars or planes from outside the car or aeroplane is possible under certain circumstances.

***

The Dog Dazer is a piece of equipment you can buy from specialist shops – I own one.

***

This is "A BEHIND THE NEWS SERIES" of Books.

Want to know more about James Dalby?
Go to:
http://www.goodnessmepublishing.co.uk

MOSCOW ASSASSIN

By James Dalby

THE STORY

The murder of Boris Nemtsov, the Russian politician who opposed the policies of the President of Russia, creates a situation where a highly placed woman with a Jewish background, working within the administrative department of the FSB, hands extraordinarily sensitive information over to the CIA in Moscow.

The original documents turn out to be assassination orders signed by the President, they also include a report on the aggressive policies decided upon by those in power affecting world peace.

The woman indicates there is a mole within the American Embassy which complicates the smuggling of the original documents out of the country. Copies will not be good enough, as DNA samples are required from the documents to prove they are not faked. Mary Clancy Head of the Moscow CIA Station and George Manning her deputy devise a method, but the Russian FSB will do anything to prevent the documents being smuggled out of the country.

Other books written by the author

Sailing on Silver

The Crowley Affair

I Am Who I Am

The Gorazde Incident *

Don't Stop the Eating

The Shanghai Incident *

The Castrators *

A Shitty Day in Paradise

The Scottish Prerogative*

Short Stories

*Behind the news series

MOSCOW ASSASSIN

CONTENTS

THE ASSASSINATION

Chapter 1

Friday 27th February 2015

Boris Nemtsov a senior politician and statesman opposed to the government of Vladimir Putin, was shot and killed crossing the Bolshoy Moskvoretsky Bridge near the Kremlin. He was walking home after a meal out in the company of his Ukrainian girlfriend, Anna Durytska, who was not harmed.

As the victim lay bleeding near the domes of St. Basil's Cathedral and the Kremlin tower behind him, the message was clear: "So die all enemies of the regime."

It happened in central Moscow at 23:31 local time on 27 February 2015. An unknown assailant fired seven or eight shots; four of them hit Nemtsov in the head, heart, liver, and stomach, mortally wounding him. He died hours after appealing to the public to support a march against Russia's war in the Ukraine on 8 March 2015, Russian authorities charged Anzor Gubashev and Zaur Dadaev, both originating from the Northern Caucasus, with involvement in the crime. Dadaev confessed to involvement in the murder according to Russian authorities, but the Russian media said he later retracted his confession.

Three more suspects were arrested around the same time but another suspect blew himself up in Grozny when Russian police surrounded his apartment block. No one believes any of the men were guilty of the crime.

At the time of the murder all the security cameras in the area were switched off for "maintenance". The only video of the incident obtained from the video feed camera of TV Tsentr studio, was some distance away at the time of the killing and only showed a stopped municipal vehicle blocking the camera.

Few believe that this method of concealing the perpetrators was a pure coincidence, it appears clear that the highest authorities had complete knowledge of this appalling act.

THE MURDER

Chapter 2

16th May 2015

The streets of Moscow were dark when Hanna Borsok was returning home from a clandestine meeting with Mary Clancy in a hotel room. She was frightened, as shortly after leaving the area of Alexeyevsky she was aware that she had picked up two followers.

They were two men in heavy overcoats and although some distance away, Hanna instinctively felt a malevolent presence. She was not far from her apartment and so she quickened her pace. Looking behind she realised that the two shadowy figures were still gaining on her and so she broke into a run.

She was relatively fit and despite her high heels, she started to pull away, as she came to a T junction she turned right into the street where she lived, but she crashed into a person coming the other way, the man she bumped into was temporarily knocked off his feet, but he recovered quickly. Hanna realised that the man's dress was like those following her, so instead of continuing past the individual, she ran in the opposite direction leaving the two followers running down the street on her left.

Now there were three people chasing her. She kicked off her shoes enabling her to run faster and she felt the sting of the cold pavement under her feet. Despite the fact it was May, the night was bitter and this helped her to run faster.

It was then that she heard the noise of a car coming down the road behind her at some speed. As the vehicle drew level, the car slowed and the driver who had wound his window down called for her to open the back door and jump in. Hanna didn't know the driver so she hesitated, as she did so, there was a burst of sub-machine gun fire from behind, Hanna was conscious for a split second as bullets entered her body, and then she knew no more. The car accelerated and took the next left turn at speed, leaving the dead woman in the middle of the road.

The followers caught up with Hanna's body and roughly searched her clothing and the small bag she was carrying.

'Damn' said the senior man who still held the smoking sub-machine gun, 'she doesn't have anything on her.'

'Which means,' said the third man, 'that she has already handed the stuff over.'

'Christ,' swore the one with the gun, 'the shit will really hit the fan if we don't find it.' He pulled a mobile phone from his pocket and swiftly punched in some numbers. The phone was answered, 'it's Andrei here, the traitor has been dealt with, but there is nothing on her.'

There were some expletives from the person on the other end. 'I suggest Andrei that you find where she has left the package, or more importantly who she has given it to. I assume the traitor is dead?'

'Yes, she was getting away, so I'd no choice.'

'Right, I'll arrange to get the body picked up from where you are; I've your coordinates from your phone signal. Send one of your colleagues to search her apartment and...'

One other thing,' Andrei interjected.

'Yes?'

'There was a car that tried to pick her up, we may have hit it, it was travelling fast, but we got the number.'

'Okay, give it to me and I'll have it checked out.'

Andrei gave the number and the phone connection clicked off.

THE UNUSUAL GIFT

Chapter 3

Saturday 9th May 2015

Seven days before the incident of Hanna Borsok, Mary Clancy was sitting in her office at the United States Embassy in Moscow.

Mary was the highly thought of head of CIA station. A career diplomat, forty years of age, blond hair always worn swept back, which accentuated her strong bone structure with a body that a model half her age would not be ashamed of possessing.

It all began when Mary decided to accept an invitation to one of the inevitable cocktail parties that senior diplomats often had to endure. Normally Mary dodged most, but it had been noticed and it was suggested to her that she ought to be seen and more importantly mix with those from other western embassies.

This one, hosted by the Russian State to celebrate their Victory Day and connected to the end of the Second World War, was held on Saturday May 9th. The President of Russia was expected to attend.

Mary, although not divorced lived separately from her husband Denis Clancy, so she asked her number two, George Manning to join her.

George Manning had joined the State department after spending eight years in the US Air force as a top gun pilot latterly on F-16 Fighters. He was welcomed because of his extensive experience in the military and his first posting had been to Ukraine. George was married with two children of school age. A good-looking man, tall with dark hair, and blue eyes, which perhaps harked back to his Celtic ancestry.

The weather on the day was cool but dry and the sight of the sun indicated a promising summer.

Once in the Kremlin, Mary soon separated from George as she made polite conversation with her opposite from the British Embassy. Most of the conversation centred on the murder of Boris Nemtsov, but as expected, no resolution had been achieved and although some people were arrested for the foul act, no one really believed they were the real killers. Political assassination in Russia is common for those who annoy the ruling class.

It was just before Mary was leaving the party that it happened, she had signalled to George that she was about to go, and he was wending his way across the floor towards her, when a middle-aged woman bumped into her to the extent that Mary almost dropped her empty champagne glass.

The woman was most apologetic and having made sure that Mary was not hurt, she disappeared into the crowd of revellers.

George had seen the incident, and asked if she was okay. Mary smiled, 'well I don't think I've been stabbed with a drugged or poisoned needle,' she laughed, remembering the old KGB method of assassination, 'probably the woman had drunk too much.'

'Not unusual with the Russians,' answered George, 'are you ready to go?'

'Yes please,' answered Mary. They walked out of the stuffy smoky atmosphere, smoking was still allowed at government functions. Mary took a breath of clean air. 'Ah, that's better,' she said, as they walked towards the embassy Limousine. 'Say George, do you feel like a coffee, there's a Shokoladnitsa Bar just across the road and we could have a quick chat about the latest gossip?'

George agreed, and Mary told the embassy driver to meet them outside the coffee bar in about half an hour.

The ordered coffee came when they were in the middle of discussing the Nemtsov murder. Mary opened her handbag to extract a tissue and came across an unfamiliar piece of paper. She looked surprised and pulled it out of her bag, looking quizzically at George as she did so.

The paper was hand written and as Mary read the contents on the page, she became deadly serious.

'Problem?' asked George noticing Mary's change of demeanour.

'I'm not sure George, here, look at this,' she handed the page over to him.

George put on his reading glasses and scowled at the paper as he read it.

'My God,' he said, 'this is dynamite, but can it be true?'

Mary considered what George had said. 'Well, it puts a lot of strange happenings into perspective, if you think about it.'

'Yes, I agree,' said George, 'on the other hand it could be a trap.'

'Hmm, but what would be gained from a trap? Simply that I would be sent home in disgrace, perhaps, but the ungodly wouldn't achieve too much, simply create some diplomatic embarrassment, which would be over in a couple of weeks, no George this has the feeling that this woman is for real, and if she is, what should we do about it?'

George handed the paper back. 'Well, the signatory is Hanna Borsok, that's a Jewish name incidentally. I know of her, she's a senior administrative assistant working for the FSB and she indicates in the letter that she is sickened by the murders carried out by the State. In particular, the murder of Boris Nemtsov, who incidentally had a Jewish background,' he continued, 'she claims to be able to obtain possession of the original orders made against several political and other assassinations signed personally by the President. She also claims that she has access to a secret plan of destabilisation and aggression throughout the whole of the western region, including the invasion of the Baltic States and for substantially increasing Russia's influence by various means in the eastern Mediterranean.

'The most immediate concern though is that she accuses our Ambassador in Moscow of being a Russian spy. She goes on to say on the other side of the page that she can't copy the documents because of the high security but is prepared to hand the originals over to you personally in return for an agreement that she be spirited out of Russia to the USA.'

The embassy driver showed up at that moment.

'Look, George, this is too serious to leave, call your wife, tell her that you've been called away and will be late. We'll go back to my apartment, which I know has been cleared by security for bugs, we need to sit down and work out a plan, we can no longer trust the embassy walls.'

George nodded, and took out his mobile phone.

After George had made his call, Mary turned to him 'I've told the driver that we're walking back, the less embassy staff knows the better.'

George agreed, knowing that she lived less than a mile away.

It took them about twenty minutes to get to her apartment and noting the obvious FSB security man nearby Mary commented, 'that should get them talking,' she smiled as she opened the main door to the apartment block.

Mary's apartment was on the top floor and when they reached there, via the elevator, she opened her external door with a special secure key and an eye scanner that was set into the outside wall. Once inside she fixed them a drink and they both sat on the comfortable lounge sofas with a coffee table between them.

Mary took a sip of her Bourbon. 'Okay, you know something about Hanna, and for the moment let us assume that what she is offering is not a trap. She's said that she'll book a room at the Cosmos hotel, which is opposite the VDNKh Metro Station. It's one of Moscow's largest hotels, and presumably, one could easily get lost in there. She's written that I should ask for Maria Korosonova. She will be there for one night only, which is next Saturday 16th May and she'll expect me between 20:00 and 21:00 hours. She's insisting it must be me; she'll not open the door to anyone else. Should anything go wrong, she'll cancel the booking and find another way of contacting me.'

'Okay,' said George, 'let's assume you go to meet her there, and you're given the papers she is promising, you'll need to assess they are original documents. To do that you'll need to take a copy of the President's signature and if that looks right, we can subsequently check the DNA from the paper, as we have his DNA on file. Then the question is what we do with them? I assume the package will be quite bulky.'

'We can take them back to the embassy and put them in the diplomatic bag for Sunday delivery,' answered Mary.

'Okay, but let's assume something goes wrong,' said George, 'and she's rumbled, but you're in possession of the package?'

'Good point George, in such a case, assuming our Ambassador is working for the Russians, I couldn't return to the embassy with them, but would have to get out of Russia "toute suite", I clearly couldn't fly out as even with a diplomatic passport, they would almost certainly relieve me of the package.'

'Well,' said George, 'they'd probably expect you to catch the train from Moscow to St Petersburg as that is by far the fastest route out other than by an aircraft. You could get the ferry to Helsinki from there, there's low security on the ferries,' George screwed his face up, 'but that route is too obvious and I would suggest instead that you consider travelling Moscow to Belgorod. The ungodly would consider that would be the last place you would head for as it's too near a war zone, I've some old friends in Donetsk in Ukraine who could meet you there and get you across the border, but it would be safer for me to do this rather than you.'

Mary nodded, 'Yes, you may be right, but I've more clout than you, and the last thing the CIA would want is their Moscow head of station to be lost somewhere in the Russian hinterland, if something went wrong our masters would be more likely to get me out, no George, this would have to be my risk. In any case, being a woman will not concern the Russian separatists so much as a man'

'Hmm, I'd like to think about that, but let's hope nothing goes wrong, if it does, we need to be prepared, you'd need a Russian passport, you speak the language fluently, so that wouldn't be a problem, but in the event of you absconding, you need to alter your appearance. Your hair is blond...'

'Blond grey,' Mary corrected him.

'Whatever, it would need to be dark, and I suggest you obtain some hair dye from a pharmacy well away from this apartment block.'

Mary nodded. 'Okay, we can put "operation fly away" in place, now let's assume that everything goes to plan, how do we get Hanna out?'

'Leave that with me,' said George, 'I'll make all the arrangements, if you tell her that I'll be following in a car when she's left the hotel, once I've established that she's not being followed, I'll pick her up before she reaches her apartment, and get her to a safe house.'

Mary nodded. 'Now,' she said, 'let's look at a situation where it's a trap.'

'Okay,' said George, 'we'll get two of our marines, out of uniform, to keep an eye on you, just in case. If they move in the heavies, they'll provide you with protection and contact me and I'll immediately put in a protest to the Russian government.'

'Right, now we need to consider what we do regarding the Ambassador, if she's working for the other side, it could be tricky,' Mary bit her lip. 'There are a number of things that have gone wrong recently which I couldn't quite put my finger on and I admit I've had my suspicions. There's a rumour that she is close to her Russian chauffeur and there is no doubt that our lady Ambassador is very friendly with the head of the FSB. There have been several reports sent back to Washington that were decidedly pro-Russian, particularly the argument she put up in the last report I saw, saying that she thought sanctions were wrong and that Washington should look at the Russian position in a more favourable light.'

On the following Monday May 11[th,] Mary was in her office when George Manning knocked and entered the room. Mary's office was on the third floor of the American Embassy. It was large and packed with an enormous number of books, atlases, reports from colleagues and personnel files. Her back was to the window with a substantial desk in front of her. Although there were two comfortable chairs in front of her desk, she preferred to talk to guests sitting on a long couch in one corner of the room, with a small table and a further two comfortable chairs opposite. There was a large television nearby, a bank of phones on her desk and a small teleprinter, which clattered away as they spoke. The inevitable computer was the main item on her desk along with a picture of a young girl, who she never referred to; George understood it was of her daughter who had died at a young age.

He sat down opposite Mary who'd moved to the couch, he told her that he had a problem.

Mary raised her eyebrows, 'go on.'

'Perhaps we could go for a short walk?' George raised his eyebrows and mouthed "bugs".

Mary agreed, and they left the embassy together via the main door. Once outside the complex, George spoke as they walked down Bolshoy Deviavinsky Pereulok towards the river.

'It's further to our discussion on Saturday evening Mary, in my opinion there's no way you can commit yourself to this trip.'

Mary smiled, and answered surprisingly, 'Yes, I've reluctantly come to the same conclusion,' she said, 'but give me your reasons first.'

'Well for a start, you're a woman, and I feel that you wouldn't stand a chance in a war zone, it's not that you're incapable of managing,' he added hastily, 'but your place is here, at least at the start, to see the operation through. If our suspicions are right regarding,' he tilted his head in the direction of the Ambassador's office, which was at the top floor of the embassy, 'then whoever goes must have someone with real clout here to ensure that the person with the package has some protection. There's something else...'

Mary looked at him quizzically.

'You're very well known, and despite any disguise, it would be abnormal for a woman of your age to be travelling on her own in that area, and they would be looking specifically for a woman.'

'Yes, okay George, I reluctantly accept your assessment, but then who....?'

'Me, I'm the obvious one, I know the people in Ukraine, and although my Russian is not as good as yours, I can get by. My experience in the military will stand me in good stead too. My suggestion is that I take Hanna with me, she'll be safer that way and as a couple, we might have a better chance.

'It's important that you meet her at the hotel and then you can hand the package over to me. On the following Monday morning you can cover for me by telling the Ambassador that you've asked for me to investigate a certain problem in Saint Petersburg, which should throw them off the scent for a time. If I run into real trouble, I can contact you in an emergency.'

'How would you do that?'

George took his mobile phone out of his pocket, 'I'd call you, and you'd be able to see my location even if I couldn't speak. You'd know if I called you that I had a major problem.'

Mary looked up at the clear blue sky, seemingly deep in thought, 'yes, but I wouldn't know the type of problem you were facing.'

George nodded, 'okay, why don't we go by numbers, 1 means I've been captured before reaching Ukraine, 2. That I'm in Ukraine but not out of the war zone, 3. I'm captured in Ukraine or 4. I can't get a safe passage out of the area. I'll keep your number in the machine with the number 1 ready, just in case and then change it to number 2 and so on.'

'Hmm, okay George, you've convinced me. Make sure you take your battery out of your mobile though as that would lead them to your location. If you must call, you can re insert it.'

They turned around and started to walk back towards the embassy.

Mary continued, 'when I find out Hanna's room number, I'll go to the bank of elevators and indicate it with my fingers. When I get up to her floor, I'll hang around until you arrive via another elevator, it's important we're not seen together. If we see there are any nasties around, we immediately abort, agreed?'

George nodded as they reached the embassy steps.

'If you then wait in the hotel corridor, I'll pass the package to you as soon as I come out of Hanna's room and I suggest you find a way out of the hotel without using the front entrance. Perhaps you could recce that before next Saturday? I'll ask Hanna to wait for fifteen minutes before she leaves so you have time to get the car, but make sure you don't pick her up straight away, make absolutely certain she's not being followed.'

When George got home that evening, he told his wife that on the following Saturday he was preparing for a special mission. 'For your sake, I can't tell you what it is, but it means me disappearing to Saint Petersburg for a few days.' He lied deliberately knowing that if anything went wrong his wife would be able to confirm truthfully where he'd gone.

'How long will you be away George?' she asked. He smiled, 'how long is a piece of string?'

She laughed, 'Oh, it's one of those secret assignations again is it, is she blond or...'

'Actually, she's blond, but not as beautiful as you my dear,' he joked.

For the rest of the week George was quite busy. He spent some time handing over his responsibilities to his number 2 and then he bought a train ticket directly from the Oktiabrskaia Station in Moscow, which was where he would catch the train to Belgorod.

He paid cash so that no indication of the purchase would appear on his computer or credit cards. He then bought golf clubs and an overnight case from a sports shop, and spent some time adapting the former with a seamless false sleeve hoping that the gap was large enough to conceal the papers he was to carry.

He arranged to procure a false passport from the embassy's special operations division, showing that he was a member of OSCE (Organisation for Security and Co-operation in Europe), and part of the team carrying out a special monitoring operation in Ukraine.

George also received false papers giving him special accreditation, which he hoped would give him a modicum of protection if challenged. Because this department was under the jurisdiction of the CIA office, he told the man in charge that under no circumstances should he divulge the passport details to anyone other than Mary Clancy. 'Not even the Ambassador,' he warned. In addition, George would carry a US passport giving his name as Timothy Shaw, the same name as his OSCE passport.

He also arranged for a passport for Hanna, using a photograph taken of a similar faced girl some ten years younger. The passport was dated appropriately and she became a Ukrainian citizen from Donetsk.

George was uncertain about carrying a gun but decided to take one as he could legitimately claim that it was for protection only.

He then drew out US$5,000 from the treasury department and 50,000 roubles equal to about $800. He carefully packed most of the currency in the lining of his case. Finally, he drew a debit card out in the name of Overseas Operations Inc, a dummy company owned by the CIA, which he could use in an emergency. He knew there were considerable funds in that account, should he need to use it.

He sent a message to his contact in Donetsk via a public phone box, using an old code instead of his name, and said that he expected to meet him in Belgorod Station at approximately 10.35 hours on Sunday 17th May, and that he would be carrying some very important documents. He arranged with Mary that he would leave the embassy pool car in a certain street near the Kurkskaia Station, which is the station for St Petersburg and get a cab for Oktiabrskaia Station at the other end of the city.

Mary agreed to get the car picked up by a member of the embassy staff, but only the following Monday morning.

George then bought a ticket to Saint Petersburg in his own name and paid for it with his credit card.

Mary had spent some time in the week creating a report regarding certain matters of interest in Saint Petersburg in case she was asked to account for George's time. Although she was not directly responsible to the Ambassador, she reasoned that being evasive would perhaps heighten the Ambassador's suspicions, particularly if she knew what had been taken.

On the Friday before travelling, Mary and George went over the complete plan. 'Okay,' said George, 'this is what I'm going to do after I reach Donetsk. I'll contact my opposite number in Kiev and establish the best plan of action for me to get up there. Once I'm in Kiev, I can get a flight to London and then on to Washington and I hope to be there within seven days, i.e. by around 24th May.'

Mary nodded, 'how will you contact someone in Kiev, bearing in mind that you could be compromised if the call was picked up by the FSB security?'

'I'll have to rely on my friends there, I'm sure they'll have a method of communicating.'

'What do you want me to do from here?' asked Mary. 'You'll have to keep your head down,' answered George, 'any call you make from here will almost certainly be monitored.'

Mary nodded, 'but if you run into trouble?'

'Hmm, I tell you what, why don't you fly to Kiev once you know that I've crossed the border, you'll be in a stronger position to help, if help is needed. You can obviously tell your opposite number what is going on once you're in a secure environment.'

'Good idea George, fortunately I don't need the Ambassador's permission, she working for the State Department and me the Central Intelligence Agency, so that's what I'll do.'

'If we can get these original papers to Washington and they can determine they are what they appear to be, all the Russian plans will be laid bare and we'll be able to expose the crimes perpetrated by the President, via the United Nations, so that the world will be fully briefed,' said George.

'Yes, but once they know you have them, the shit will fly, as you indicate, it totally compromises the Russian position and the President in particular. Be absolutely sure George, that once they suspect you, they will move heaven and earth to stop you getting away, so for all our sakes be careful.'

'I will Mary, and if the American Ambassador is working for the Russians, we can "kill two birds with one stone".'

Mary smiled, 'or we'll leave her in place and feed her the information we want the Russians to hear.'

THE SWITCH

Chapter 4

Saturday 16th May 2015

"The best-laid schemes o' *mice* an '*men*. Gang aft agley, An'lea'e us nought but grief ..."

All appeared to go well on the day, Mary drove to the underground car park of the hotel and caught the elevator up to the lobby. She went to the desk and asked for Maria Korosonova. The receptionist telephoned the room and told Mary that Maria had requested that she should go up to room 3115, 'it's on the third floor,' she explained.

George had entered the hotel from the main entrance and although he scanned the area for FSB operatives, it was so busy in the lobby area that it was impossible to make a clear assessment. He walked over near the bank of elevators to wait for Mary to appear, he pretended to read a copy of Pravda, which he'd brought with him. Mary didn't acknowledge him on the way back to the elevators but when she was waiting for one to appear where she was standing, George walked past behind her and with one hand behind her back, she showed three fingers.

George then went to another elevator and pressed the button.

Within a few minutes, Mary was knocking at the door of 3115.

'Who is it?' asked the muffled voice behind the door.

'Mary Clancy, Hanna,' she looked down the corridor both ways, 'and there is no one else here,' she lied, noticing George coming out of an elevator.

The door opened, and Hanna looking very frightened let Mary in closing the door behind her.

Mary studied Hanna she was a middle-aged woman with dark curly hair which had a touch of grey. She had a darkish complexion and Mary thought she would have been quite attractive when she was young, but her skin was blemished and she was dressed in rather dowdy clothes, surprisingly she wore smart high-heeled shoes.

The room was quite large, most of it taken up with a king-sized bed and a couple of armchairs. On the bed lay some documents, Mary first checked the bathroom to ensure there was no one hidden there and then she checked the large wardrobe, satisfied there was no one else in the room, she crossed over to the bed and flipped through the papers.

There were several assassination orders signed by the President, another lengthy report on the future policy plan for Russia 2015-2020, which Mary noticed contained names of various countries including the Baltic States, and some others which surprised her. She then came across reports received from someone code name "Ohio" who was clearly a senior person in the US Embassy. Mary then remembered that the Ambassador had been born in Ohio. There were some other reports, but Mary was keen to get them to safety, so she rolled them up and fixed an elastic band, which was lying on the bed, went to the door, and opened it. George was strolling by and she gave the documents to him, he promptly put them into his case among the golf clubs he was carrying. He then went to the emergency staircase and walked down to the basement where he let himself out of an emergency door. He heard the alarm go off as the door opened. Walking quickly to his car parked nearby, he put the golf clubs in the boot and drove off.

Mary went back into the room. 'Okay Hanna, this is what you have to do now. Go out of the hotel and across to the VDNKh Metro, it's only about 400 yards away. Catch the train to Sukharevskaya. When you get there, walk south down Stretenka and turn right on Bolshoy Sukhavevskiy. A friend will pick you up in a car there; his name is George and he has everything arranged to get you out of the country. Whatever you do, don't go back to your apartment.'

'But I've things I need to collect,' protested Hanna.

Mary nodded, 'yes you may have, it's your call, but to return to your apartment is taking too much of a risk.'

Hanna shrugged, 'I only took these documents last evening,' she said, 'so it's highly unlikely they will be missed until Monday.'

Mary shrugged; she knew that as soon as George had parked his car he was going to walk back and watch the front of the hotel, if Hanna didn't go to the Metro Station, he would assume that she had gone back to her apartment to pack as it was quite near the Cosmos Hotel situated off Tserkornaya Gorka.

She and George had discussed such an eventuality and prepared for it.

Mary quickly left Hanna, suggesting to her that she not leave for at least another fifteen minutes. As she opened the room door, she heard a faint alarm still ringing and she assumed that George had exited by an emergency door at the back. As she went to the elevator, the ringing stopped. She took the elevator straight down to the underground car park and walked towards her car. She was briefly conscious of two men in heavy overcoats walking by and as she quickly got into her car, the two turned and hurried towards her. Mary switched on her engine and was pulling out of the parking slot but she was too late and the last thing she was conscious of was two guns firing in unison. Although killed immediately, her foot still on the accelerator she careered into another parked car in front creating a huge noise.

One of the men opened the driver's door and searched Mary's body, the other looked in the car but found nothing. They knew that she hadn't had time to put anything in the boot and as people started to run towards the car and others congregate nearby, they left the scene.

Hanna left the Cosmos through the front doors and walked past the Metro entrance heading straight for her apartment, a fatal mistake. George followed behind her at a distance, but he realised she was being tailed. He then went back to his car and drove to a spot where he would be able to see Hanna turning into the road where she lived, he parked without lights.

He saw her appear around a corner and she was running. He saw the collision with the man walking the other way he drew level with Hanna, opened the driver's window, and shouted to her to get in the back.

Hanna looked at him terrified, a look that George was to carry with him for many years afterwards. He felt rather than heard the bullets hitting the car, and then a scream from Hanna as she fell away. George knew that to stop would be useless, so he gunned the engine again and sped around the corner out of sight. He found that his hands were shaking as he drove out of the complex of apartments and towards the metro.

As his brain started to get into emergency mode, he was gratified that his hands had stopped shaking. He knew that it was likely that the number of his car had been taken as he'd switched the lights on before he took off, hoping that they would serve to dazzle the pursuers, which they did for a moment in time.

He drove into a quiet side street, extracted his golf bag and an overnight bag, which contained sandwiches his wife had prepared for him, then walked to the Metro Station getting a ticket for Oktiabrskaia Main Line

Station. He looked at his watch, he had only about 35 minutes before the train to Belgorod left the station, but as he already had a ticket, he reckoned he would just make it.

He did, and as he climbed up the step into the carriage, the train started to move. He found the inspector in charge of the sleeper cabins who escorted him to his cabin and gave him his key. As he got into the cabin, he began to wonder how Mary had got on. He quickly undressed and climbed into the single bunk.

He felt the train increase its speed as it pulled out of the station, and then started to consider what sort of reception he would find at Belgorod if things had gone wrong. Remembering Mary's caution, he swung out of the berth, grabbed his mobile phone, and with a pin from his case took out the battery. He then got back into the berth and after telling himself that he was now committed and there was nothing he could do until his arrival in Belgorod, he slept soundly.

The next thing he knew was he was conscious of a loud urgent banging on the door of his sleeper.

THE FSB

Chapter 5

Colonel Sherepov was sitting at his desk at the FSB headquarters in Lubyanka Square in Moscow on Saturday 16th May. Sherepov had spent the beginning of his career in Stalin's KGB and had managed to keep his head, when many of his colleagues were losing theirs. He had thinning sandy coloured hair, a slight man with careful eating habits; he was a vegetarian and didn't drink alcohol unless the circumstances demanded it. His director had once written a report on him stating that this man was very loyal to the State, being highly efficient having the reputation for persistence, once he got his teeth into something, he rarely let go. He was not married, which had caused some consternation among his peers, but it appeared that he had no sexual desires for either men or women; he was married to his job.

He had just arrived in his office and was expecting a busy schedule due to the murder of Boris Nemtsov. There had been several muted protests in Moscow, but so far, nothing serious. Noting the date on his calendar, which sat on his desk showing the previous days date only, he leaned over and changed the date from Friday 15th May to Saturday 16th.

Colonel Sherepov didn't usually work on Saturdays but the current situation demanded his careful attention. After writing a report for his masters, it was about midday when he called for some items from the administration department, only to find that there was no one there. Irritated, he walked down to the next floor and let himself into the secure area. He identified the filing cabinet where the Nemtsov file was kept, but on opening it he found the document he was looking for was missing. He frowned, wondering if someone had misfiled it, he looked in another file, and again the document pertaining to that file was missing too. Sherepov, now thoroughly concerned, began looking in other files; each one was missing the document he was looking for. He went back up to his office and telephoned the senior administrative officer who was about to leave for a football match. 'Vladimir, I'm looking for the 'X' files (X was a code for assassination) and I can't find them, where should I look?'

'Ah, they are in the individual files under the target's name sir.'

'Well, they are not there Vladimir, so where else should I look?'

Vladimir frowned; he was annoyed at being called on a Saturday, particularly as it was a big football match for his team.

'Well, that department is run by Hanna Borsok and she's usually extremely efficient, I'll call her and get back to you.'

Sherepov put the phone down, and started to work on other things when the phone rang.

'It's Vladimir here sir, I've just rung Hanna's phone, but there's no reply.'

'Did you try her mobile?'

'Yes sir, no reply although I left a message.'

'Hmm, tell me Vladimir, wasn't Boris Nemtsov Jewish?

Vladimir thought for a moment, 'yes, I believe he was.'

'And Hanna Borsok, is that not a Jewish name?'

'Yes sir, but she's been cleared by security at the highest level and has worked for us for almost twenty years...'

Sherepov frowned, 'I don't care if she's been with us for fifty years, the files appear to be missing and I smell a rat, get over here immediately and contact a couple of filing clerks from Hanna's department, I want a full search done.'

Vladimir felt a cold sweat; he knew that if sensitive files were missing then it would be his head on the block. 'I'll come over immediately sir, and on the way, I'll call in some help, I should be there by,' he looked at his watch, 'it's just after 12:00 I'll be there by about 13:00.'

Two of his staff arrived before him as Vladimir lived outside Moscow. Sherepov set them to work, and by the time Vladimir arrived, they had already found some more areas of concern.

Sherepov asked one of the assistants to bring Hanna's file from the personnel records and was studying it when Vladimir knocked at the office door.

'Come,' called Sherepov.

Vladimir entered the room looking extremely worried. 'I am afraid it's very serious sir, the files that are missing are all the presidential 'X' files, also the file on 'Ohio' and the report on the policy decisions agreed regarding our expansion of interests marked "Operation filtration".'

Sherepov looked aghast at Vladimir. 'Do you realise what this means Vladimir, if those files get into the wrong hands, my job, your job, and the security of the state is in jeopardy. This is not just very serious, it's a fucking disaster,' Sherepov was raising his voice.

Vladimir started to shake with the shock; if the files remained missing, he knew what would happen to him.

Sherepov became icy cold, 'very well Vladimir I'll deal with you later, keep your staff looking and bring me another report within the hour. In the meantime, we need to take some action, now get out of my sight.'

Once Vladimir had left the office, Sherepov picked up his phone to the security office.

'Yaroslav.'

'Yaroslav, its Colonel Sherepov here, we have an emergency, are you the duty officer?'

'Yes sir,' he answered.

'Right, get up to my office now, and bring with you a list of the number of "soldiers" who are available for immediate duty.'

Within five minutes, there was a knock on the door of Sherepov's office and a man came in without waiting for an answer. He stood to attention opposite Sherepov's desk and saluted, 'Captain Yaroslav reporting for duty sir.'

'Sit down Yaroslav, how many trusted men can you call together quickly?'

'Fifteen sir, if you need more, I can call others in but it will just take a little longer to organise them.'

'Okay, Yaroslav, here's the problem. We suspect that one of our senior administration staff has stolen some very sensitive files. She would almost certainly have taken them home last night. Now, I suspect that she may be meeting someone to hand the files over.'

'American, British?'

'We don't know at this stage, but it's imperative that these files are recovered and quickly. Here are her details, it contains her home address and there is an up to date photograph. Get three men over there now, but don't apprehend her, just follow to see whom she meets. I suspect she'll probably move away from her apartment and meet in a restaurant or hotel.

'It may be that she's already left her home, in which case keep an eye on local hotels nearby, my bet is that it's the Americans.' Sherepov threw a folder over his desk. 'Here's a file containing senior people working in the US Embassy here. I'm afraid this has to be an 'X' case, no one may be left alive to talk about what they have seen do you understand?'

'Yes, of course sir.'

'And Yaroslav, none of your men should look at the files should they be recovered, they are that sensitive, if you suspect any of them have done so, they should be shot immediately.'

'I'll give very strict instructions, and deal with anyone who exceeds their authority.' Yaroslav stood up and saluted.

'Keep me informed Yaroslav, this is my mobile number and remember, if you need more resources, let me know.'

Three men raced to Hanna's apartment, but by careful surveillance they established that she was not there, so they stationed themselves in adjoining streets, so as catch her on her return. Four men went to the nearest hotel, which happened to be the Cosmos, two in the huge lobby area and two in the car park below. Six other men placed near the American and British Embassies kept watch with an additional man at the entrance to the VDNKh Metro.

Having organised that, Yaroslav put out a general alert with photographs. He stated that if anyone was seen, he be contacted immediately, but no one should be apprehended.

He then sat back and waited. Fortunately for George, his picture was not among them.

The security men in the lobby of the hotel asked if anyone named Hanna Borsok had booked in, but they learned that there was no such name on the register. They showed a photograph of Hanna, and the people on duty didn't recognise her. If they had been fifteen minutes earlier, the girl who dealt with Hanna would have been on duty, but she had recently been relieved.

It was about 20:30 when they heard an alarm sound, but it switched off quite quickly, they didn't ask what it was. The senior man's mobile in the lobby rang. He received news of the shooting of one of the people on the 'hit list' when driving her car out of the underground parking area.

Both men rushed to the elevators and pressed the button for the car park. About a minute later, Hanna appeared and walked through the front door unseen. Unfortunately, she decided to go back to her apartment.

It was later that evening when Yaroslav reported to Sherepov. 'We have established that the person killed in the car park was Mary Clancy of the American Embassy,' and as you know, we managed to stop Hanna Borsok getting away, she was shot trying to get into a speeding car.'

'And the car, did we get its number?'

'Yes sir, it's one of the pool cars from the American Embassy, we found it later near a Metro station. It was empty, but had several bullet holes in the rear.'

'No idea who was driving?'

'No sir, he drove past our men at speed, it was definitely a man, but that's all we know.'

'The files?'

'No sign of them I'm afraid. Could they have been posted?' asked Yaroslav.

Sherepov shook his head, 'no they wouldn't have had time, and in any case these files would be far too important to post.'

'They could have copied them,' argued Yaroslav.

'No, their value is that they are original, they will need to get them out of Russia, so we now need to consider who and how.'

Yaroslav thought for a moment. 'Well it's doubtful they would try and fly them out as they would almost certainly be discovered in the security checks. I've given orders to all airports that all baggage, including checked baggage has to be searched thoroughly.'

'I've also asked the airports to report anyone from the American Embassy leaving with a diplomatic bag to be detained pending your permission to release them.'

'Hmm, the people we're dealing with would have thought of that, no they are not going by air, they wouldn't try getting out by road but just in case ensure that all vehicles are thoroughly searched including large trucks and their cargo.'

'How about the train?' Yaroslav asked.

'That's the most likely,' agreed Sherepov, 'but in which direction?'

'I suppose the most likely is through Saint Petersburg, it would be relatively easy to smuggle papers across via the ferry to Helsinki.'

'Or there is a large American Consulate there, and they would have a diplomatic bag facility,' said Sherepov, 'but as you say you've catered for that eventuality.'

'But if they were going to use the diplomatic bag, they could have done that from Moscow,' said Yaroslav looking puzzled.

Sherepov told him that wouldn't have happened, but didn't explain why. 'Try St. Petersburg, that could be our answer, we must assume that it's someone from the American

Embassy who has the documents, so do a further check on all the personnel files of people working for them and send copies of their photographs to all stations, but make St. Petersburg the priority. All the American diplomatic bags must be opened,' he saw the look on Yaroslav's face.

'Make the excuse that there's been a terrorist plot to infiltrate diplomatic bags, they'll scream and protest, but we can live with that. However, it's unlikely that a diplomatic bag would be sent over the weekend unless they were trying to get rid of something urgently, so we would be quite in order to search them.'

When Yaroslav had gone, Sherepov dialled a number, a woman answered. 'Are you on a secure line?' asked Sherepov.

'Yes, but you shouldn't be calling me, we have special arrangements for contact, you should know that,' said the woman irritably, 'besides its past midnight.'

'Yes, I know,' said Sherepov, 'but this is an emergency and we need your help now.' He emphasised the word "now".

Sherepov then related what had happened. 'There's someone from your operation who has these files that not only compromise the State, but you too.'

There was silence at the other end. 'Did you understand what I said?' asked Sherepov.

'I'm thinking,' was the retort. 'Okay so Mary's been eliminated, as has this other person, did you say her name was Hanna?'

'Yes.'

'Right, then almost certainly the person who has the package would be George

Manning, Mary's number 2. He's no fool, but I'll give you his mobile number, you may be able to trace him through that, providing he hasn't taken his battery out that is.' She looked into her phone book and gave the number to Sherepov.

'Okay, Ambassador, we'll give that a try, but assuming he's read the file he won't be in touch with the embassy, so perhaps you could call the consulate in St. Petersburg and warn them that he should be arrested for murder.'

'That's no good,' she said, 'if he has the file, he could soon persuade them otherwise, no I'll just ask them to inform me if he contacts them. I'll go into my Embassy tomorrow, as its Sunday there'll be no one around so I'll have a dig.' A thought just struck her. 'I've just remembered, I was told of an unauthorised request to send two marines to the Cosmos hotel yesterday, I cancelled the order, but now I know what that was all about.'

'Okay,' said Sherepov, 'I've had an instruction from above that we have to put out that Nemtsov was killed by the CIA to destabilise the Russian State, no one else will believe it, but most Russians will and that's what counts.'

'You realise that I'll have to put out a strong denial?'

'Of course, but I mention it so that you're ready for it,' answered Sherepov.

'I'll also have to put out a statement about Mary Clancy. What's your story going to be?'

'In the first instance that she was murdered for her money, but by tomorrow morning it will be discovered that she was involved with the Nemtsov murder, that will tie in with the CIA.'

'Goodnight,' the American Ambassador put the phone down and immediately started to make plans in case things went wrong.

BELGOROD

Chapter 6

Sunday 17th May 2015

The banging on the door of George's cabin continued unabated, heart in mouth he reached for his automatic pistol and with it held behind his back he stood well away from the door.

'Yes,' he shouted.

The person behind the door shouted back in Russian, 'we've arrived in Belgorod; you have to vacate your cabin.'

George lifted the blind behind him, sure enough, it was light and the train was in the station. He heard the man walking down the corridor banging on other doors. George sighed with relief and quickly got dressed. He put the gun away, lifting his golf bag on his back and opened the door. He'd realised that the package was far too bulky to put in his overnight case as incongruous as it was, he had to continue with the golf bag. He later found a larger case and switched the documents over.

He was relieved to find there was no one around, so he poked his head out of the cabin door, picked up his case with the golf club bag and left the train.

He'd arranged to meet a man at a coffee bar opposite the station, he studied the outside of the place for any sign of the ungodly before walking over to it, he sat down at a small table and ordered a light breakfast with coffee. Just as the waiter brought the food to him, he felt rather than saw someone looking intently at him. The man got up from his table and went over to where George was sitting, 'excuse me' he said in Russian, 'do you have any Turkish cigarettes?'

'No, only Russian I'm afraid.'

The man smiled, 'my name is Gorky, I've been sent to collect you; Ivor and Leond are outside the town, they are wanted by the security forces so they couldn't show their faces here. I'm afraid I've some bad news for you, Mary Clancy was killed last night, and it's all over the news this morning.

George felt sick in his stomach as he assumed that Hanna was dead too, but the FSB would be unlikely to put that out on the news. 'I'm very, very sorry to hear about Mary, she'll be a great loss to us.' He remembered that he'd promised to send her a coded message once he was over the border, so one thing less to consider he thought. 'How did Mary...'

'Die?'

'Yes,'

'She was murdered in the underground car park of the Cosmos Hotel, and now the FSB are putting out that the CIA killed Nemtsov, and citing Mary Clancy as the instigator, so the Russians are up in arms about it, at least those that believe the story. However, I do have some good news for you, Ivor has been in touch with the American Embassy in Kiev and so they know roughly where you are and what you're carrying.'

'I hope he used a secure phone,' answered George with a sinking feeling.

'No, he sent a courier and we know he got through, because he sent us a coded message.'

'Thank goodness,' said George.

He finished his breakfast quickly and paid his bill, walking out to the car with Gorky. He was rather disappointed to see that it was an old Lada, in quite a bad state of repair.

'Are we going to Donetsk in that,' said George pointing at the wreck in front of him.

Gorky laughed, 'no, but to come to town with a good-looking vehicle would have looked odd, so I'll take you to Ivor and you can switch. The drive to Donetsk will take you about five hours, but it may be longer because of road blocks,' he added.

George piled his clubs and bag into the back of the Lada and they set off heading west.

It took only half an hour to reach a motel where Ivor and Leond were waiting.

As they drew up in the old Lada a well-built man with grey hair cut short and a fearsome moustache came out of the main door of the motel followed by another taller younger lean looking man with dark hair who sported a small beard, both were dressed in a Russian

47

army uniform. 'George, it's been too long since we last met, and your pretty wife and beautiful children are well I hope, it's so good to see you.'

They hugged, 'They are all well Ivor, thank you, and thank you for coming to collect me. I don't know how I could have considered this journey without your help.'

George moved across to the other man, 'Leond, it's good to see you again,' they shook hands.

'Let us go inside and talk for a moment,' said Ivor, 'there are some problems ahead of us.' George nodded and followed him into the motel where they found some comfortable seats away from the reception desk; they ordered coffee. Gorky excused himself saying he had to get back to Belgorod, and George thanked him for meeting him off the train.

'Take care George,' he said on parting, 'you're moving into dangerous countryside,' and with a wave he was gone. The coffee came and Ivor took over the conversation.

'What papers do you have George?' he asked. George told him.

'Ah yes, you indicated that when you called, so you have papers to prove that you are a member of OSCE, but papers don't always help in this environment, it's this that one has to rely on.' He touched his hip where George noticed he kept his gun. 'The problem is that there are Russian soldiers, mostly professional and disciplined except on a Saturday night,' he grinned, 'but the rest are an undisciplined rabble, mostly out for what they can get from this war. They do respect a professional soldier though, and that is what we are going

48

to be. I,' Ivor pointed to the uniform he was wearing, 'am a Colonel in the Russian Spetsnaz on special duties, Leond is a Captain and you my friend are a special OSCE negotiator who is guaranteed safety under our command. I've a letter signed by the Minister of Interior giving me special authority. The papers are false of course, but it will get through most checkpoints, and those that are more difficult, we may have to shoot our way through.

'The vehicle we're using is a Gaz 233014 Tigr 4x4 which we apprehended from some guy who took a wrong turning.'

'It was the last thing he did,' grinned Leond.

Ivor nodded, 'It's armoured, and I've placed a divisional flag on the outside, just so they know that we are someone important.' He laughed, 'most of these guys on the road blocks are Ukrainians and they don't know who is who, so we should be able to bluff our way through.

'The problem we have is we can get you to the other side of Donetsk, but after that it becomes much more difficult for two reasons, 1. There's still fighting on the front and 2. There are a lot of professional Russian soldiers there, and we could have problems with them. So, we plan to get you to a "safe house", and I do mean a safe house as you'll see.

'Now let us discuss tactics, I assume you are armed George?'

George surreptitiously pulled out his pistol.

'That's no bloody good, George, I've a Heckler and Koch sub-machine gun, which came with the vehicle, it has some real stopping power, and the magazine is full by the way.' He passed over a carrier bag with the gun inside it.

'Keep that by your side. Leond has an Uzi; he prefers them as do I. If you must shoot, shoot to kill, you won't get a second chance. I've got some stores on board, so we don't have to go shopping when we arrive.'

Ivor looked round to Leond 'Let's go,' he said.

The drive was uneventful until the border, when their identification passes received a cursory look.

They passed through without any problem. Both Ivor and Leond were conspicuous in their military uniforms and George had changed in the back of the car into a NATO type uniform, which he had brought with him. It was lighter than the Russian type.

'Only another 2 and a half hours,' said Ivor, 'keep your fingers crossed.'

The next roadblock was about an hour down the road, and when the guard noticed the insignia on Ivor's arm, he beckoned them straight through. The problem came at the next checkpoint when they received an order to get out of their vehicle.

Ivor showed them the paper allegedly signed by the Minister. They ignored that, probably because they couldn't read said Ivor afterwards. Ivor snarled at the Sergeant in charge, 'we have no intention of climbing out of our vehicle,' he said, 'do you not respect rank soldier?'

The Sergeant, a surly looking man said he had his orders.

'And who gave you those orders?'

'Major ....'

'A Major and you dare tell me, a Colonel to disembark, you must be mad, fetch your Major to me now,' he barked.

The Sergeant slipped a round into his rifle and looked threatening. 'He is not here,' he said.

'Leond,' John said quietly in English, 'let the Sergeant see your Uzi, not as a threat, you understand, but he should be aware that we are armed.' George moved up from the back with his gun in view. There were six soldiers at the checkpoint, and Ivor reckoned that with an armoured vehicle, they could fight their way out if necessary.

'Sergeant,' he said smiling, 'I have no wish to have a fire fight with fellow comrades, let alone kill them. I tell you now that I am ordering you to stand aside, otherwise we are going to disagree, and if I don't kill you then my regiment will,' he moved his arm nearer the open window so that the Spetsnaz insignia was in plain view.

One of the Sergeant's companions suggested in a heavy Russian/Ukrainian accent that he should let the vehicle through, 'we're not going to get anything out of these guys, frankly their fire power is greater than ours and they have an armoured truck.'

The Sergeant wavered, and then nodded his head in the direction of Donetsk. Ivor gunned the engine and shot past him.

'Phew,' said George, 'that was a near thing.'

Leond turned to George, 'the problem is if you get out, you're are likely to lose your vehicle and maybe your life too, that's what it's like here.'

They travelled through two more check points but had no further trouble and as Ivor drove to the north west side of Donetsk; they passed streets of ruined buildings, most of which had been destroyed by the shelling. George remembered Donetsk as a thriving community with shops, restaurants, and bars. The place was now deserted.

They reached what looked like a fortified farmhouse surrounded by a thick wall that Ivor referred to as the safe house. Ivor drove the Gaz into the compound and Leond jumped out and closed the substantial gates they had just driven through.

As George climbed out of the vehicle, he commented on how surprised he was that such a place was still standing, particularly after travelling through the ruins of buildings as they passed through Donetsk.

Ivor laughed, 'It actually belongs to my family, but it was the temporary Head Quarters of the Ukrainian army; they were allowed to leave without a fight, so it was completely abandoned and because it's now so far behind the lines, no one wants it.'

'So, what now?' asked George?

'We stay here until it's safe to move,' answered Ivor,

'And if it isn't safe to move?'

'We develop another strategy,' answered Leond with a laugh.

George nodded, 'I do have a problem,' he said, 'I need to get these papers very quickly to Washington and that has to be via the American Embassy in Kiev.'

'Okay,' said Ivor, 'let's go inside and get a fire lit it's getting cold and after some food we can discuss our next move.'

'Yes, that's sensible,' said George, 'but don't we need a guard or sentry?'

Leond laughed, 'they are already here,' he remarked, 'they just disappeared when we arrived because they weren't sure who we were. You see we didn't start out with the Gaz, it was acquired on the way to meet you.'

George looked through the dirty window and noticed three men with sub-machine guns and one with a bazooka patrolling the grounds.

'There are another three in the barn at the back, they do four hours on and four hours off,' Leond explained.

A fire lit, they sat down to some stew that Leond had made, and it tasted surprisingly good. Afterwards they sat around the fire and discussed their position.

'How much does Kiev know,' asked George?

'Only what you told me in your signal,' said Ivor.

'Hmm, I've got to contact Kiev so that they know the importance of what I have, what would be the best way of getting there?' asked George.

'At the moment it's impossible, the man I sent barely got through with his life, and if your documents are as important as you say, you can't possibly take the chance of being captured,' argued Ivor.

'If I use my mobile from here, the call would almost certainly be picked up and that would compromise our position, of course e-mail is not safe either, even if encrypted, which I couldn't do anyway,' said George gloomily

'What about Morse code?' Leond said.

George looked at him in amazement, 'you mean you have that facility here?'

Leond grinned, 'yes it was left here by the Ukrainian army, it's hidden in the barn.'

George had noticed that there were no bulbs in the light sockets, 'electricity?'

'No, we have batteries and they are fully charged.'

'Do you know your Morse code?'

Ivor laughed, 'Leond belonged to a Ukrainian signals unit.'

'Okay', said George, 'but could the Russians pick up the signals from here?'

'Yes,' answered Leond, 'but it would be a surprise and then they'd have to triangulate the signal, unless you're writing a novel, there's no way they would locate on one send only.'

'Unfortunately, the only thing we cannot do is to tell them where you are,' said Ivor, 'as we don't have encryption facilities, which means everything is sent in the clear.'

'Okay,' answered George, 'what would be the best time to send?'

'When the buggers are asleep,' answered Leond, 'say about 3 a.m., tomorrow morning. What you must do George is compress your message while still getting the importance of it through, if you say you're with Ivor it may be that someone there remembers where he used to live. And if you can't get out, they'll have to come and get you.'

'How'd they do that?' George asked.

Leond shrugged, 'there are ways,' he said, 'the Americans have plenty of assets if it's important enough to use them.'

At 3 a.m., on Monday 18th May, George handed Leond the message, it read: To: Head of CIA Station USA Embassy Kiev.
Code 6523XYW.
Have extremely important compromising original Russian assassination documents stop. Also original of plan for aggression in Europe stop US Ambassador in Moscow suspect, stop. Need to reach you urgently but local difficulties prevent me doing so. Stop.
Donetsk.
'The code identifies me,' explained George, so no need to spell out who it's from, just give the code.'
He handed the message to Leond, who had already set up his machine. The signals man at the other end in Kiev was on the ball and he picked up immediately, the message took only seconds to send and Leond received a code confirming receipt.
'You didn't give coordinates as to where we are?' said Leond.
George shook his head, 'no, because Ivor indicated that the message was sent in the clear and if picked up, we would all be in hot water.'
Leond nodded, 'yes I suppose that's wise, but I've added a message that we will be listening in at the same time for five minutes each morning. I doubt if anyone else would have picked that up.'

THE CHASE

Chapter 7

Monday 18th May 2015

The American Ambassador got to her office early on Monday morning on 18th May and noted a number on her phone, which she recognised. She switched off the recording apparatus and switched the scrambler on her phone, then pressed a button to call the number.

'Sherepov.'

'You rang.'

'Ah, Emilie,' he called her by her first name, 'thanks for returning my call, I've some information for you, can we meet?'

'Time and place?'

'The usual, say 10:00 hours.'

'See you there.'

She put the phone down.

She thought about her search of the CIA office in the embassy the day before, which drew a blank. She considered her situation if she was exposed, it was not a happy thought, and made her even more determined to stop George Manning before he could cause any damage.

At 09:45, she took her own car to a certain underground car park and walked across to a large limousine with blacked out windows. Checking that no one was around she opened the rear door and climbed in.

Sherepov greeted her with a shake of the hand. 'I've some news for you, we thought we'd caught George Manning yesterday, as our people in St. Petersburg arrested a man who had similar features, unfortunately he was shot dead, and afterwards we discovered he was a Swede on his way back to his country.'

'Embarrassing, I suppose you've told the Swede's that he was killed by some half-drugged bandits, who were intent on robbing him?'

'Something like that,' Sherepov answered, 'but your George Manning was clever, he didn't go to St. Petersburg, although he'd bought a ticket to go there, he took a train to Belgorod.'

The Ambassador screwed up her face, 'Belgorod, what is he doing down there?'

'Well, when you think of it, it was the last place we would look as most people would head away from a war zone, but not our George. It's quite clever really, as Western Ukraine is in chaos now, so he'd have a good chance of getting lost there.'

'So, he went to Ukraine?'

'Yes, and this was confirmed when we picked up a message sent last week to a contact in Ukraine telling him or her that he would be arriving in Belgorod by train, unfortunately the message only reached me this morning when the communications department realised that it may have been sent by the same man we were looking for. It was further delayed because of the report from St. Petersburg that he'd been apprehended.' He added.

'So even the FSB have their screw ups.'

Sherepov ignored the acid remark. 'More importantly, we picked up a message yesterday, which I also received on my arrival at the office this morning. It's a transmission sent from the Donetsk area, here's what it said.' Sherepov handed her the message. 'Unfortunately, because we didn't realise that Manning had gone south, our people in Donetsk were not informed of our interest until late last night.'

'So, you've picked him up?'

'It's not quite as easy as that,' explained Sherepov, 'the Donetsk area is large and the situation is fairly chaotic there, as the message was transmitted by a professional, there was no way they could get a directional fix on exactly where it was transmitted from. One thing we do know though is that is he in a region we control, and if he moves, he's almost certainly going to be caught.'

Emilie Dixon scowled, 'well, he's obviously taken his battery out his phone, as there's no indication from our end as to where he is.' she said. 'I should have realised that Ukraine would be a possible area he'd consider, as a Russian speaker, he was posted there a couple of years ago.'

Emilie thought for a moment, 'okay, I'll send the Kiev Embassy a damning report on

Manning, and suggest he should be arrested if he shows up there, but frankly if he does, and he has those papers with him, he'll not have much difficulty in convincing them of my complicity. Unless you want to lose a valuable asset, he must be killed before he reaches Kiev.' She looked at Sherepov.

'I agree, and to that end I'm travelling to Donetsk by plane this morning to lead the search, don't worry Ambassador, if all is lost you know we'll look after you.'

'Like you did with Philby?' She was referring to the infamous British spy.

Sherepov smiled, 'that was the KGB, and we do things differently nowadays.'

'And who was running the KGB at the time? I do believe it was a man called Putin.'

Sherepov smiled, 'a little early for Putin, it was Vladimir Semichastny who was responsible in those days.

***

Sherepov arrived in Donetsk late on Monday afternoon and almost immediately met with the Russian commander in the area, a General Shalovorich. Over a glass of vodka, Sherepov told the General that he had come to Donetsk on the request of the highest authority. Shalovorich knew precisely what he meant by that.

'There is a CIA man hiding in your area General, it's essential he be found as he has documents stolen from the FSB that would compromise all our plans. This is the man,' Sherepov handed over George Manning's file.

The General opened it and took out the photograph, calling his secretary as he did so. He handed it to her. 'Have this copied immediately and sent to all units, also instruct a copy of the picture be placed in public places such as restaurants and so on. I suggest a reward of,' he looked at Sherepov and raised his eyebrows, '$5,000 US dollars to be paid to anyone giving information that leads to his arrest.'

Sherepov nodded in agreement.

'It shouldn't take long comrade, the people here are hungry for cash, and if he's been seen, we shall soon know about it.'

'That's fine General, but I also need a search detachment to scour the area, piece by piece.'

'And where do I get the troops to do that, there's a war on you know.'

Sherepov nodded, 'you can call in another thousand troops, and I'll obtain a Presidential order to allow you to do that.'

The General nodded in assent. 'Very well Colonel, and who is to lead such troops?'

'I am General, this man must be found, which is why I'm here, and not in Moscow.'

THE BRITISH INPUT

Chapter 8

Monday 18th May 2015

The American Ambassador to Ukraine was studying a report he'd just received from his opposite number in Moscow, when his secretary entered. 'Excuse me sir, but Jim Wallace wants to see you urgently.'

'Sure, show him in,' said the Ambassador, putting down the report he'd been reading on his desk.

'Good morning Mr. Ambassador,' said Jim Wallace as he walked into the room.

'You can drop that crap,' answered the Ambassador, who happened to believe that Jim Wallace; who was head of the CIA Station for the entire Ukraine, was arguably the most efficient officer in the service, and that being so, they were extremely friendly, unusually so, as the CIA and the State Department didn't always see eye to eye.

Bill Cummins an ex-military Colonel of the marines in charge of a tank regiment had been highly decorated in the Gulf War. He was what was termed a soldier's commander, highly respected by his men and senior Generals. He'd been invalided out because of wounds inflicted during the advance on Bagdad.

In view of the situation in Ukraine, he came out of retirement to take up the position of Ambassador.

Jim Wallace was a very different type, recruited from quite a high position in the FBI stationed in Washington DC. Although primarily an administrator, he had a penchant for difficult and unusual situations; known as a man who thought outside the box, he had no fear of disagreeing with his senior officers if he felt they were wrong.

Jim laughed, 'okay Bill, but this is urgent business.'

'Go on.'

'We received this message very early this morning, which is like the one we received by courier from an old friend who works for us in and around Donetsk. It came in Morse code in the clear, which probably means that they have no encryption facility.' He handed over the plain text message.

Bill Cummins read it.

'That's real interesting Jim, because I've just received a report from my opposite number in Moscow;' he threw the report across his desk.

Jim read it. 'Well now that's even more interesting.' He sat back in his chair. 'There's something that doesn't add up here Bill, you know of course that our Head of Station, Mary Clancy was killed in Moscow on Saturday, and now Russia is blaming the CIA for orchestrating the death of Nemtsov, which is ridiculous of course, but it will find followers in Russia who'll believe it.

'Now they are saying that Mary was the person responsible. I know that's not true of course, but I've no doubt that she was somehow implicated in getting hold of the documents referred to in George Manning's message, she always was a "hands on" type of person.' He continued, 'I happen to know George very well, he was posted to this embassy a couple of years ago, he's a very level-headed guy and he did a great job for us, which is why he was promoted to the number two spot in Moscow.

'The fact that the Russians killed Mary suggests that the documents are really hot and if George has them on him, they could be dynamite, and the reason he couldn't get them out of Russia in the normal way, would suggest that there is some conflict between the Ambassador there and the CIA.

'He mentions that the US Ambassador is suspect, we don't know what he means by that, but if she's working for the other side, then by Christ, we need to sort that problem out fast.

'To sum up, my feeling is that if these documents are what he says they are, we have to get hold of 'em. Using whatever means at our disposal.'

Bill Cummins nodded, 'yeah, you're right Jim I don't know the Moscow Ambassador, although I've probably met her once or twice. The only way to clear up this matter is to get

George and his documents out, and then we can assess the situation from there.'

Jim Wallace, leaned forward, 'but how the hell can we do that Bill, we have no assets to speak of in this area.'

'Hmm, no we don't yet, but I know someone who does.'

'Oh?'

'The Brits, have just sent a training team to help the Ukrainians, but they are really SAS and probably some of the most capable guys you could wish for.'

'Ah, yes, I remember seeing the report. But would they....'

Bill Cummins interrupted, 'their Ambassador owes me one, I'll go and see him this morning and see what we can do, I've a gut feeling about this, if I'm right those documents George has will be just as important to the Brits as to us. Now, what you can do in the meantime Jim, is contact your pals in Langley and ask them if they could find out where the nearest Apache choppers can be found, and to see if it would be possible to obtain an executive order to switch them to Kiev for a special mission.'

'Are you suggesting that we send the Brits in on Apache helicopters...?'

'Hell no, we don't know where these guys are and they can't tell us because their messages are sent in the clear and so can be read, what we need is a team to go in and find them, no mean job, and as soon as we have that information, we can then send in the choppers.'

Jim Wallace frowned, 'but Apaches can't take passengers.'

'Well you're wrong Jim; there was an instance in Afghanistan where the Brits strapped themselves to the outside of the Apache to rescue a wounded soldier. Each Apache could carry up to four people this way. Don't forget their motto, "Who Dares Wins".

'The great thing about using these machines is that they are armoured and can fly at high speed at night at a low level and they are fucking deadly to anything that tries to stop them, particularly enemy ground assets.'

When Jim Wallace had gone, Bill picked up his phone and called in his secretary. 'Judy, call the British Ambassador and ask him if I could call round and see him this morning, it's urgent.'

A few minutes later, Judy put her head round the door, '11 a.m. do?'

'Great, order my car to pick me up.' Bill loved walking but nowadays it was not wise for American Ambassadors to walk anywhere, in view of potential Islamic assassins. Bodyguards now always accompanied them.

The Ambassador's car was in the underground car park under the embassy, and Bill Cummins climbed in with two other men plus the driver. It took only five minutes to reach the British Embassy, which was also in its own compound. As soon as the car was inside the gates Bill Cummins got out, strode through the entrance and ignoring the elevator, walked up to the fourth floor of the building. Because he was well known, nobody tried to stop him.

As he appeared at the top of the stairs, the British Ambassador James Winston-Jones met him. He laughed, 'my security people told me you were walking up, so I thought I'd come out to see if you needed any help,' he joked. 'Come on in Bill, coffee?'

'Great, no sugar, no milk.'

James Winston-Jones was the epitome of a British Ambassador, suave, highly educated, and thoroughly entrenched in the Foreign Office hierarchy, coming from a long line of civil servants in his family going back to the nineteenth century. James was quite young for the position he held. His 1.9 metre frame gave the appearance of being rather gangly, but his mind was sharp indicating that he was heading for substantially greater senior positions in the future.

James ushered the American Ambassador into his office where there were some comfortable sofas in front of a coffee table. 'Please, have a seat Bill, now what's up?'

Bill explained exactly what Jim Wallace had told him, leaving out the comment about the American Ambassador to Moscow.

James sat back in his chair, in deep thought. 'I would have to get permission from my boss, so it might be a good idea if you get your Secretary of State to have word, I can speak to the Chief of the Army to assess the feasibility, but I assume this is very urgent as if the ungodly find George first, then it would be all over.'

Bill nodded, 'Yeah we're probably talking in hours rather than days, I'm afraid.'

'Okay, I see that we've to act quickly but if our guys go in, how do we get them out?'

Bill told him of his idea of sending in Apaches, 'probably six of 'em, if we can get them, that really is an essential and I've got Jim working on that now.'

James made his decision, 'okay Bill I'll go with it providing you get your choppers on standby and providing our guys think it's feasible and I get clearance from London. You'll need to get a "safe field" as near to Donetsk as possible, obviously on ground still held by the Ukrainian State. We could pick up George from there with one of our Jet Ranger's and get him back to Kiev. One condition though.'

Bill Cummins smiled and raised his eyebrows.

'That you give us a copy of all the documents, and I do mean all of them,' he smiled.

Bill Cummins jumped up, 'Done,' he said. 'I'll go and get things organised, perhaps we could meet same time tomorrow when hopefully we have a "go" from our leaders.'

As soon as Bill Cummins left, James picked up the phone to the new commander of the British Forces Training Team, a Colonel Watson.

'Good morning Colonel, I've just had a visit from the American Ambassador and he has asked for our help, can you spare me some time this afternoon?' he thought for a moment, 'no, I'll tell you what, how about lunch at the embassy?'

Colonel Watson agreed, wondering how on earth the British army could be of help the Americans.

Watson arrived at the British Embassy in full uniform and was escorted up to the Ambassador's office. A drink offered and accepted and while waiting for lunch, James explained the problem.

Hugh Watson was an extremely experienced officer and had received his "red tabs" at the age of only forty-four. He'd also been in the Gulf War, and had worked with Bill Cummins during that period. As a younger man, he'd had a spell of commanding an SAS Regiment, so he was the ideal man to be in the position he was.

'Hmm, that's an interesting idea, I certainly have the right man to lead such a team, but if these documents were so important, why were they simply not sent by diplomatic bag?'

'It appears that they are so compromising that they wouldn't have been allowed out of Russia, even in a diplomatic bag. The American Ambassador told me that the head of station in Moscow was murdered on Saturday, this news will hit the newspaper headlines here tomorrow, the guy who got away with the documents was her number 2, but he's in grave danger of being found, if we know he's in the Donetsk region, then so do the other side.'

Colonel Watson nodded; 'the problem is we would need someone from the area to support us, as none of my guys have been over the other side.

'Do we know who's hiding him?'

'I believe the Americans may have an idea. George Manning is the man's name. He was posted here a couple of years ago, so the CIA station here are searching their files to see if any name jumps out to them that were in the Donetsk region. I understand they recently received a courier from one of their agents so I suspect we will learn more when we meet tomorrow, of course we don't know whether this agent is still in touch with George Manning.'

The lunch arrived, and they continued to discuss the possibilities of such an incursion. After lunch Colonel Watson said he would take the matter up with one of his team leaders for a view, and leave the Ambassador to deal with the politics. They agreed to meet at the American Embassy the next day at 11:00 hours, Tuesday 19th May 2015.

By the time Colonel Watson accompanied by Captain John Desmond attended the American Embassy, a considerable amount of preparation was under way, and Watson was surprised at the speed of approval for the suggested incursion, suggesting that the documents in question were indeed extremely important.

Bill Cummins, who made the introductions, hosted the meeting held in a large conference room in the American Embassy. 'Firstly, James Winston-Jones, British Ambassador to Ukraine, Douglas Armitage of MI6, Colonel Watson Commanding officer of the British Forces training Team, and Captain Desmond who it's suggested will lead the incursion Team into the War Zone area. Jim Wallace Head of Station for the CIA and his deputy Peter Lienster and finally myself Bill Cummins

American Ambassador to Ukraine. I would like to thank our British colleagues for offering their help to solve this problem and I confirm that we now have clearance from our respective governments to carry our plan through as we think fit. I have to say, that never in my career have I seen either of our two governments move so quickly on what may well be a complicated operation in another country. By the way, we have received the green light from the President of Ukraine himself, but he would deny all knowledge of the plan if anything goes wrong, which is why there is no Ukrainian representative here.'

'That's just as well,' said Douglas Armitage, 'Ukraine is still a very leaky place.' Jim Wallace agreed.

'Okay gentlemen, I suggest we start off with Jim Wallace, who has some interesting news.'

'Hi, everyone, yes we looked at the files created during George's time at the embassy here, and there are two names that stand out, one is Ivor Letinsky and the other a signals expert called Leond Melnyk. They did quite a lot of work together and we're certain that the transmission we received was sent by Leond as our expert said it had his "signature" all over it. If he's with Leond, it's likely he'll be with Ivor too, as they were good friends. Both these men are anti-Russian so far as we are aware.

'Now, we know that Ivor comes from an area west of Donetsk, and the last we heard of him was that he or his family owned a farm that was fortified by the Ukrainians, but when they were surrounded, they left. Now the farm, is reportedly empty, as it is quite a way from the front line. It's possible that Ivor has taken it back. I can point it out on the map for you.' He looked at Captain Desmond.

'Was that the man who sent the courier?' asked Colonel Watson.

'Yes, but at that time George wasn't with him, we suspect that George would seek his protection once in Ukraine,' said Jim Wallace. 'Because of security the courier wasn't told where Ivor was working from in case the he was captured.

'We've been informed this morning that the FSB have issued a US$5,000 reward for the arrest of George Manning, which means they know he's in their area and that tells us that he hasn't yet been apprehended. We know that Colonel Sherepov of the FSB has flown down to the area to take command of a search force consisting of over 1,000 troops, which means two things. 1. Sherepov wouldn't be there unless the matter was extremely important and 2. It'll not take them long to find our guys as $5,000 US is very attractive to the locals who are struggling to find enough money to eat, and a thousand men can cover a lot of ground quite quickly.

'Finally, we've received an executive order to procure 6 Apache helicopters direct from one of our bases in Germany, they'll be flown here tomorrow, that's Wednesday 20th. We've arranged to send some of our embassy marines to set up a temporary camp within spitting distance of the dissident area, but far enough away to ensure that the Apaches and their crews are safe. We've earmarked somewhere in the region of Dnepropetrovsk but well out in the country safe from prying eyes, and we're sending a transport helicopter which we already have here, that'll be taking the marines plus supplies and spares. We'll also be sending down a fuel truck to the site as soon as we know where it's to be located, so the aircraft can be refuelled there. The choppers will be fully armed, so no ammo needs to be transported. Once we have the coordinates of the site, I'll pass them on to you.

'The idea is, that as soon as Captain Desmond, who I understand is to lead his team, has located George Manning, the attack Apaches will fly in at night close to ground level and pick him up along with his compatriots if they want to get out. We'll be fitting special attachments to the outside of the aircraft so that personnel can be strapped to them, we know this can be done as the Brits did something similar in Helmond Province in Afghanistan.'

John Desmond laughed, 'yes they did, I should know, I was the one who organised the pick-up.'

'Gee, that's great, so you know exactly what to do,' said Jim Wallace.

John nodded.

'Okay, if you guys have any other ideas, we'll consider them, now I'll hand over to Colonel Watson.'

'Thank you, gentlemen, I've discussed this in some detail with Captain Desmond here, and I'll hand over the floor to him shortly. From our point of view, we want to be in and out fast. I've arranged for a civilian Jet ranger aircraft to fly down to the temporary American camp when it's set up to bring George

Manning to Kiev. I have also arranged with the Royal Air Force to station 6 Tornados in Kiev, and they'll give air cover for the Apache's. The Ukraine government has given permission for these planes, they'll be fully armed,' he said. 'Now I'll hand over to Captain Desmond.'

All eyes turned to John Desmond. It was noted that John who was 1 metre eighty-eight tall, was well-built and he looked extremely fit. His hair was dark, but there was noticeable grey appearing around his temples, which made him look older than his twenty-eight years. His face was square and clean-shaven and he'd a confidence about him that was apparent. The sort of man that if he walked into a crowded room would be immediately noticed, he was good looking and exuded leadership, thought Bill Cummings.

He looked up from his notes. 'The team I'll be taking will number seven people only, two Ukrainians, Bosilav and Viktor; I can't pronounce their names. These guys are purely for the language problem, one female nurse, a Molly Castle, her involvement is mainly in case of George Manning being hit, one signals expert a guy called Josh Beeton, one explosives expert, Carl Ronson, he's nicknamed "fire-lighter",' John grinned, 'and finally my number two, Sergeant Kieran McCauley and myself. We've recently received two Mercedes AMG 6x6 G-Class Wagan's. This is a lightly armoured type vehicle developed for the military, and we've been given them to test, so we'll certainly do that,' he smiled. 'they are ideal over very rough ground and are fast, important because we'll be travelling over difficult terrain once we get near the separatist area.

'We'll be carrying wireless equipment in both vehicles, tents and supplies, sub-machine guns, Anti-tank weapons, and a new system of directional spotting utilising a digital set up connected to one of our military satellites. Two heavy machine guns, one each set up on the rear of the vehicles and grenades with grenade throwers, 2 mortars with bombs and a Stinger anti-aircraft missile launcher with four rockets. We'll also be carrying quite a lot of explosives in case we need to blow up an obstacle. Finally, we'll be carrying armoured fuel tanks on the back of the vehicles. We estimate under normal circumstances the driving time to Donetsk is nine hours, however as the last few miles will be carried out over rocky ground it's difficult to know how long it will take. Barring problems, we should make it easily within 12 hours. We've already gone over the terrain and have programmed our inboard GPS systems to take us over as clean ground as possible, that is avoiding impossible structures at night. Other details are not for this meeting.'

'Thank you, Captain Desmond, now gentlemen if there are no questions, we need to determine a time line,' said Jim Wallace.

John put his hand up.

'Yes Captain.'

'We intend to set off at 20:00 hour's tomorrow evening,' he looked at his watch, that is Wednesday 20th, so that all of our travel will be made in the dark and in the separatist area, we would hope to arrive at the target by dawn or close to it.'

'Does everyone agree with that?' Asked Bill Cummings.

All around the table nodded.

'In that case gentlemen, perhaps we could meet here at the same time in two days' time, that will be Thursday 21st, to discuss the situation as it arises, with of course the exception of Captain Desmond who will be quite busy at that time.' Bill Cummins smiled. 'For the rest of us we need to have our press people get together to ensure a common story.'

When John had left the meeting to make his preparations, Jim Wallace looked across at Hugh Watson.

'Captain Desmond seems very young, apart from being familiar with the Apache, does he have any experience for this type of project?'

Watson laughed, 'Desmond was awarded the Military Medal for bravery in Afghanistan as a Sergeant in the SAS and subsequently the Military Cross as a Lieutenant after his promotion. He's an exceptional officer and will go far in the service. Of course, all officers are only attached to the SAS and he was originally from the Royal Engineers before he volunteered for an SAS posting as an ordinary soldier, it's quite unusual to have an Engineering officer as a SAS commander, but in this situation, it may well be very useful, which is why I picked him. Sergeant Kieran McCauley is also a holder of the military Medal from an earlier conflict. Trust me you could not have two better men leading this operation.'

'Thank you, Colonel Watson,' Bill Cummings smiled, 'you can be sure that we

Americans have the highest regard for the British Forces who we feel fight with one hand behind their backs due to the lack of funding, and the SAS are world renowned for their skills. I for one have every confidence in them completing their objectives. As I haven't met the rest of his team, I'd be interested to know something of their background.'

Watson smiled, 'Kieran McCauley is from an Irish family who moved to Liverpool before he was born, he's tough and looks it. The short ginger hair identifies him as a Celt but he keeps his muscular frame in trim by being a regular visitor to the gym when not on duty. Looking at him you get the definite impression he's not a man to mess with, and I assure you he's not.

'Josh Beeton is the great, great grandson of Mrs. Beeton the famous cook. Transferred from signals to the SAS about two years ago, he's a small man with a ready smile and nothing seems to faze him. He's not the smartest of soldiers from a dress point of view, and he wears his hair rather longer than the regiment requires, but he's extremely intelligent, an absolute wizard on a computer and any type of signals equipment.

'Carl Ronson, the explosives expert is naturally ribbed about his name. He's the quietest of the team and probably the deepest thinker. As his profession requires, he has a cautious nature. A man of average height, he looks and speaks like the Yorkshireman he is, his ruddy complexion could be mistaken for a Dales farmer, which is what his father is.

'Molly Castle is a fully trained nurse, I'd put her age around thirty. She's quite plain to look at, but has shown exceptional qualities in the field, and has saved many lives.

'I'm afraid I know very little about the two Ukrainian's except they were strongly recommended to us by our security people, who they actually work for. I've talked to both separately and I would judge them extremely capable if there's trouble. They hate the Russians, and Bosilav's sister lost a leg by their illegal bombing of civilian areas.'

THE RIDE

Chapter 9

Wednesday 20th May 2015

John Desmond and his men were involved for most of Wednesday in stocking the vehicles and by 15:00 hours, they were in bed asleep. They took off as planned at just after 20:00 and the 5.5 litre turbo charged v8 engines made cruising at 80 M.P.H. a doddle, with 586 bhp the power was equal to most super cars on the road.

Once they left the tarmac road, the advanced GPS system accurately indicated the route the vehicles should take over the rough ground avoiding the worst of the terrain. Because it was linked to speed, the vehicles would slow when there was difficult terrain ahead and speed up again afterwards. Kieran McCauley commented on the psychological difficulty driving in the pitch black despite wearing night glasses, not knowing whether one was heading for a cliff edge. 'I hope these bloody GPS systems know where we're going,' he said, 'damned if I do.'

The new system allowed them to travel more safely without lights on the rough ground and as the vehicles were relatively quiet, they didn't run into trouble until about 30 miles north of Donetsk, when they saw a flare go up in front of them bathing the vehicles in a bright light. Shortly afterwards they heard rather than felt bullets whistling around them. 'Turn around and head back until we're out of that bloody light,' ordered John.

Kieran did so, but then the GPS system was telling them to turn around. 'I don't think the designers made this GPS system for going back, I've no idea where the hell we are going.' said Kieran noticing that the vehicle behind was following faithfully. Once well out of range, John took out his small laptop and called up the satellite. He then used the infra-red and heat indicator to determine what was in front of them. It looked like a small outpost, but he could see a few people climbing into a vehicle and that vehicle was heading towards them, he then saw a second vehicle, much bigger but couldn't tell what it was. He told Kieran to turn the engine off and he opened the door, running back to the vehicle behind and told them to do the same. He then listened. A tank has a very significant noise caused by the chains clanking. He decided it was a tank, but moving very slowly.

'Okay guys just follow us, we're going up towards the left and we'll stop in about 500 yards. Josh and Carl use your camouflage netting to cover the vehicles, take a couple of AT-4 Anti-Tank Bazookas and station yourselves on the ridge to your left,' he identified the direction with his powerful torch, 'you may be able to get a rear end shot from there,' he added.

'Kieran, you and Borislav move away from the vehicles with your heavy machine guns and the rest of us will go down the hill to deal with any survivors. For fuck sake make sure your firing line does not cover where we are.' With that Carl and Josh disappeared into the night, John, Viktor and Molly crouched down just as the first vehicle appeared. There was someone with a large light on the top of what looked like a lightly armoured 4x4 vehicle. Kieran fired a burst from the heavy machine gun and there was a yell as the light shattered. Another flare went up, but due to the camouflage, there was nothing immediately visible to the crew in the 4x4. They were firing wildly and John realised that professional soldiers didn't operate these weapons. Borislav fired the first AT-4 and it hit the truck squarely. Two men, who got out of the back, fell under the machine gun fire. Just then the tank appeared and the driver seeing the burning wreck of the truck, unwisely turned the tank round to head back the way he'd come. The second AT-4 fired and the tank stopped momentarily and then exploded. There were no survivors. It was all over in a matter of minutes.

John stood up, 'okay guys, well done, get the kit into the vehicles, and let's get out of here.' He looked at his watch it was 04:30. Thursday 21st May. When returning to his vehicle, he again fired up the computer and did a complete scan of the area. He noticed what appeared to be a larger camp about five miles further on, so he adjusted the GPS to go around, giving the area a wide berth.

They then set off again keeping well to the north. Dawn was approaching and John, struck by the beauty of the hilly area they were in, wondered why people could be so stupid as to fight over such a huge area that was completely wild.

As they were manoeuvring round the side of a hill, he noticed an enemy helicopter some three miles away. He indicated for them to stop, hoping that the camouflage paint would be enough to stop them from being seen by the aircraft, but the chopper altered its course and came straight towards them. 'Okay, usual drill we all get out and wave to make them think we're friendly, you Kieran hide behind the rear vehicle with the Stinger and let him have it when I shout. Don't miss, we won't have a second chance.' The helicopter was an old Hind 24, obviously one commandeered from the Ukrainian Army. Desmond noticed one of his team spreading out a Russian Flag on top of the lead vehicle.

The chopper came on and then turned side on to take a better look. It was the last look any of them took as John shouted 'NOW'. Kieran fired the Stinger, which hit the chopper full in the centre of its fuselage. It exploded in full sight, bullets flying everywhere from its crippled armament. It crashed down the valley in front of them, making a huge noise as it went.

'Good shot Kieran, but these guys are not truly professional as they wouldn't have come so near, so the next encounter may be more difficult, particularly as it's now light.'

The flag folded up, they moved off. 'Do you think they reported our position?' asked Kieran.

'Well, we have to assume they did,' answered John, 'my feeling is that we should find a valley and go to ground, there's too much fire power around, and we'd be sitting ducks in the light, particularly from jet aircraft.'

'How far do you reckon we are from our target?' asked Kieran.

'About ten miles, but of course we don't know if the target is where we need to be.'

Kieran nodded, 'Look why don't we split, you, me, and one of the Ukrainians, perhaps Borislav plus Carl, walk to the target, carrying the explosives we need plus an AT-4 and Stinger with our other kit. We leave the vehicles hidden with Josh, Viktor and Molly, as she would slow us down, and if we find the target is positive, we can come back and move off after dark. At least half of the party will get some sleep.'

'Okay, that sounds to be a sensible plan;' agreed John, 'I'll talk to the others.'

Everyone agreed that Sergeant McCauley's idea was the best one. The first essential was to get the vehicles into a hidden situation, and they quickly found a suitable gorge where they were able to cover the Mercedes vehicles firstly with the camouflage nets and then cut gorse bushes. They covered the vehicles to such an extent that they were not visible from within a few metres, never mind from the air.

To facilitate communication, John decided that they should take one of the radios. He arranged they would make contact at 20:00 hours that evening if for whatever reason they couldn't return.

He opened his computer and scanned the area for other signs of life, but it appeared barren, so they set off towards the target heavily laden. Later, just as they were breaking cover, they heard jets overhead and they threw themselves on the ground. The jets soon disappeared, and John continued with his group, stopping for ten minutes after every two miles or so. About ten minutes after the last stop they heard explosions and looking back they saw a huge plume of smoke spiralling up from where they had left the others.

'Oh no,' said Kieran, 'you don't think...'

It was about an hour later that they heard further explosions behind them. John frowned as he wasn't aware of any aircraft around and wondered what the second explosion was.

Fifteen minutes later they reached a ridge, and below them was the fortified farm that was their target. There was no sign of any movement, so they walked cautiously down the hill towards it, stopping behind a large bush.

'Hold it,' said John, 'this could be a trap. I'll go down on my own and reconnoitre the area.'

Kieran demurred, 'no sir, that's my job, you're in command, so if there's a problem you'll have to get the guys back.' He didn't wait for an answer, but shedding all but his sub-machine gun, he ran down the hill towards the farm.

John told Carl and Borislav to get ready to offer covering fire for Kieran should he need it.

McCauley gingerly opened one side of the double gates and passed through; as he did so two burley-armed men grabbed him on both sides. His sub-machine gun was taken from him and he was frog marched into a nearby building.

Ivor was sitting with George Manning when Sergeant McCauley entered the room.

Ivor got up, 'Well, well, what have we got here?' He said in perfect English.

McCauley's eyes darted around the room and settled on George Manning, he fitted the face with a photograph they'd all studied.

'Mr. Manning, I assume,' He felt a little foolish remembering from his school days the meeting between Stanley and Livingstone.

George stood up, recognising the British uniform. 'And who might you be?'

'I'm Sergeant McCauley sir, SAS Regiment, we've come to get you out, but we needed to pin point where you were, as no one was certain.'

George nodded, 'yeah, we couldn't take the chance of using the radio to let you know our coordinates as that would have given our position away, I'm very glad to meet you Sergeant,' he held his hand out. 'I think you can let Sergeant McCauley go now,' George smiled at his captors, who released him.

'I assume you have some colleagues with you?' said Ivor.

'Yes sir, my commander, an explosives expert, and a Ukrainian, are awaiting my signal, they are up on the ridge,' George pointed in the general direction.

Kieran asked for his sub-machine gun back, but his captives appeared reluctant to part with it. Kieran turned to Ivor, 'look, if I appear at the gate unarmed, they'll assume the worst, tell your "dogs of war" that I'm not the bloody enemy for Christ sake.'

Ivor laughed, 'you have to excuse my men they have fought many battles, and are not particularly trusting.' He barked an order to the man with McCauley's gun. They handed it back to him, he immediately checked that the safety catch was on, but he noticed that they kept their fingers on the triggers of their own guns.

He walked out to the gate, and waved to the others to come down. They noted that he was still armed but John told Carl and Borislav to walk behind him and be ready for a trick.

Once inside they met George Manning, and he introduced Ivor and Leond. As they sat down, they were all offered strong coffee.

After all the introductions, John moved to a nearby table and pulled out his map.

'This is what we're suggesting,' he said addressing everyone in the room. 'The overall priority is to get you,' he looked at George, 'out with those important documents; everything else takes second priority, including us.' He grinned. 'Now we've got 6 attack Apaches coming down from Germany, standing by to fly in, obviously it would be preferable for them to come in as soon as possible, probably tomorrow night, to be precise. They'll be flying at close to ground level, so they'll be under the radar and God help anything that tries to stop 'em. There'll be cover from half a dozen British Tornadoes flying high, in case of problems...'

Ivor held up his hand. 'Can I advise that the Tornados don't fly?'

Desmond raised his eyebrows.

'They have the new Su-35's down here; the Tornados would be no match for them.'

Desmond nodded, 'well I'm not an aircraft expert, but we'll pass that on when we make contact, thank you for the information Ivor. So, the plan is to fly in the Apaches, and depending on how many we need to evacuate, will depend on how many land.'

Ivor frowned, 'but the Apache is a fighting machine, it doesn't carry passengers...'

'Normally it doesn't but they'll be specially equipped with gear so you'll be able to strap people to the outside of the machine, I'll go through the drill with you later, don't worry it's been done before, I've done it.' He smiled at George's expression. 'They'll be carrying warm clothing including hoods and goggles and the documents will fit in the cabin of the lead chopper, everything else is expendable, even you George.' He grinned.

'Thank you very much,' said George.

'Okay, that's the plan, but it's important that it appears that you've been killed George and the documents destroyed, so to the world the mission will be broadcast as a regrettable failure, there are some good reasons for this...'

George nodded, 'yes that's essential, but my wife is still in Moscow...'

'Okay I've been told that your personnel department have dealt with that, they have a village in Florida where they take wives and children of field operatives on risky missions, so I suspect she'll be well looked after, although she'll be worried, I've no doubt.

'Now, one last thing, we left some colleagues with the vehicles, and as we heard explosions behind us, we're naturally worried, so we're going to have to return as soon as it's dark to see if they are okay, and if so bring them in.'

'Hang on sir,' said Kieran, 'we asked them to stand by at 20:00 hours on the radio, perhaps we should wait until then at least.'

'Sure, we'll do that, but we'll still need to bring 'em in, as we can't broadcast our position.'

'Providing they are still alive,' said Kieran with a worried look on his face.

'Yeah, well we'll see,' said John, 'in the meantime we all need to get some sleep,' he looked at Ivor. 'If you've some spare bunks somewhere, we'd like to kip down as we didn't get any rest last night.'

THE TRAP CLOSES

Chapter 10

Thursday 21st May 2015

Sherepov had been diligent in his searches, thoroughly scouring each designated area before moving the troops in. He'd received many false starts from those wishing to benefit from the reward, but to no avail. He'd now covered 25% of the Donetsk area which was the south-west and was about to start on the north-west. He reckoned that the hiding place would probably be on the western side, nearest the Ukrainian border. He was constantly receiving calls from his superiors for faster action as they knew the longer the search took the more chance of George Manning escaping.

On a visit to the local General's office Sherepov happened to see the latest reports from the north-west area. His attention was transfixed on two reports, one being the massacre, as reported, by a small unit of Army separatists who found the remains of a blown-up vehicle, a tank destroyed and several bodies. There was a further report of a helicopter shot down after sighting two strange looking army vehicles.

He frowned and grabbed a map of the area noticing that the first encounter was about 20 miles north west of Donetsk and the helicopter only about 12 miles north west.

He went outside and called in his Major, the man who was directly in charge of the searches.

'Look at this Karloff; I think we may be seeing some sort of rescue attempt. It's too much of a coincidence, what do you think?'

'I agree sir, the direction appears obvious, but it's rough country up there, if they came over in the dark, they must have had some sort of guidance system, because if they came in daylight, they'd have been spotted.'

'Well, what would you do if the trip took a little longer than anticipated, and you were found a sitting duck in daylight hours?'

'I'd run for cover sir, and stay there until night fall.'

'Yes, that's what I may do too,' Sherepov answered slowly. 'But this doesn't appear to be a Ukrainian incursion, the way these two incidents were dealt with was professional and they were well equipped, even with a Russian flag, it says here, one of the last things the pilot reported before being hit. Now it maybe they have gone to ground, there are plenty of gorges in that region where you could lay up for days without being discovered, but let's run a line from where the first incident happened to the second incident.'

'That runs straight into Donetsk sir, on the north west side,' answered the Major.

'Yes, it does, on about 120 degrees but that doesn't mean to say that our quarry is actually in Donetsk.'

'What would you like me to do sir?' asked the Major.

'Let's assume that they were headed straight for Donetsk, take a line from the second incident and add ten kilometres either side,' Sherepov jabbed his finger on the map. 'Search that area today; I've a feeling that we might be lucky.' He looked up and smiled. 'Keep in touch Major, I'm going to take a small aircraft and have a look around those gorges.'

The Major saluted, 'we were going to the region anyway to see if there were any survivors from the helicopter crash, so we'll just widen the search.' He walked out giving orders for the troops to be loaded onto the trucks and to move off immediately.

Sherepov told his driver to take him to the airport and on reaching there, he enquired if there were any small planes that were still serviceable. He was told that there was a small De Havilland Chipmunk aerobatic aircraft owned by a local businessman, but it hadn't been used for a while.

'That will do, have it fuelled for me, and get me a key.'

'I'm sorry sir, but I would need to get the permission of....'

Sherepov showed him his identity card. 'I'm in a hurry, do as I say please.'

'Yes, of course sir, I'm sorry sir, I didn't realise.'

Sherepov nodded, 'as quickly as you can,' he said smoothly.

Within 30 minutes, he was in the air headed for the area on the map.

When he reached it, he headed to the top of the nearest gorge, gained some height, and then turned the engine off gliding down the gorge silently. Near the end, he gunned his engine and headed for the next gorge. It was during his flight through the third gorge that he saw a woman in uniform looking up at him and then running for cover. He gunned his engine after noting the coordinates, gaining height in order to get a good signal.

He called up the General's office call sign. When they answered, he said, 'this is Colonel Sherepov of the FSB, please ask the General to send 2 Su-35's to the following coordinates,' he relayed them to the operator. 'I've spotted an incursion and believe there may be vehicles under camouflage. I saw one person in uniform that appeared to be British, probably SAS. Please acknowledge.'

The message sent straight to the General in charge who picked up a phone and asked if any of their troops were in that area. Told there were none, he phoned the air force H.Q. and gave the order.

Two Su-35's were in the air within a few minutes.

A NEAR RUN THING

Chapter 11

Thursday 21st May 2015

Molly Castle, the nurse left behind with the
vehicles was returning after a call of nature,
when she heard a small aircraft approaching.
The aircraft appeared to have been gliding and
so it was almost on top of her before she heard
the engine revving. She looked up in to the sky
just as it flew over their position. It was flying
very low, she saw a wing dip and could see the
pilot quite clearly. She ran for the vehicles
under the camouflage.

She heard the aircraft increase its speed as
it flew out of the gorge.

Josh, the radio operator had heard it too,
he looked at Molly. 'Did you look up at the
plane?'

'Yes, I saw the pilot quite...'

'Oh Jesus,' he exclaimed, 'Molly you never
look up, you'll be surprised at how easy it's to
see an upturned face from the air...'

He turned to Viktor the Ukrainian. 'We
need to move, now. You take the other Merc,

and follow me.' Josh wasted no time, he roughly pulled off the brush and took off the camouflage netting, folding it quickly and stowing it in the vehicle. Then getting into the driving seat he started the engine. He pulled out a map of the area from the glove box and studied it as he was driving forward. He looked in the mirror, Viktor was just moving off.

'Where the fucking hell can we go,' he said almost to himself. He then noticed a cleft in the rock about half a mile further on and put his foot down. The Mercedes was superb over rough ground and they covered the distance within about ten minutes. Josh drove into the cleft backwards and put the hand brake on, jumped out and guided Viktor in beside his vehicle. Together they covered both vehicles with the camouflage nets, and then they cut more bush until the vehicles were invisible from the gorge. Josh told Viktor to join them in his vehicle.

'Okay you guys, we should be safe here for a while, but you can be sure that they'll be sending in ground troops...' At that moment, they heard the scream of jets overhead and multiple explosions further up the valley where they'd been.

Josh was looking at the map again. 'As I was saying, you can bet your life they'll send in troops to confirm what they have bombed, and when they find nothing, they'll start looking, which means that we're unsafe where we are.'

'The problem is,' answered Viktor, in broken English, 'if we break cover we'll be spotted, it's a clear day out there.'

'Yeah, you're right Viktor. I'll tell you what we'll do. We offload the stuff from your vehicle except for some of the explosives left behind by Carl, and we'll drive back to the original place and blow the bugger up.'

'But if they find no bodies?'

'They'll assume that we were all blown to pieces.'

Viktor grimaced, 'what if the helicopter we shot down reported two vehicles?'

'Well, they would take time to establish that, and most people in that position would get the hell out of the area, whereas we will be only half a mile away. I know it's not perfect Viktor, but do you have a better plan?'

Viktor didn't.

'Look, by the time they get troops here it will probably be late in the day, if we can sit it out until night, we can then move depending on what Captain Desmond's needs are.'

'Okay, let's go, which Merc is to be sacrificed?' asked Viktor.

Josh grinned, 'yours, which is the one with the least kit, now let's get the stuff moved over.'

It took them about half an hour until they were ready to move. 'Molly, I suggest you stay here, as we'll move faster without you, don't leave the area whatever you do, and if you want a pee, do it within the confines of this cleft', said Josh unkindly.'

They took the camouflage off and drove out turning right up the gorge. It took rather longer to reach the old area, which was now completely devastated. The bombs had not all been accurate and part of the cliff face had

94

been hit which meant them taking quite a large detour.

Once there Joshua and Viktor set about laying explosives around the vehicle and the external fuel tanks. It took them over half an hour to complete the job, and when they'd finished, they paid out the fuse wire for about fifty yards.

'Okay, are you ready?' asked Josh.

Viktor was looking at the fuse wire. 'The problem is that if they see that, or the remains of it, they'll know that it was deliberately blown up by us.'

'So, what's the alternative?' asked Josh.

'We use a shorter fuse that doesn't go any further than the Merc.' he answered.

'And blow ourselves to Kingdom Come?' answered Josh.

'Not necessarily,' said Viktor, 'if we twist the fuse wire around the vehicle several times leaving a reasonable gap between the windings, it will take just as long to get to the explosive.'

Josh saw the sense in what Viktor was saying. 'You're a clever bastard, aren't you?' He said grinning, 'okay let's do it.' They unwound what they had done and re set the wire round the chassis and roof about ten times. 'Make sure it's fairly loose,' said Viktor, 'so the body doesn't interfere with the burning.' When they had finished there was a very short piece of fuse wire at the end, Joshua lit it.

They both ran like goats down the track and were pleased when they reached a corner, which would protect them from the blast. They waited and waited, nothing happened. 'Jesus,' said Josh, 'the fuse must have....'

There was a huge explosion and they saw parts of the Mercedes hurtling past their position as they stood with their backs to the cliff. They also noticed some rocks dislodged above them so they moved away quickly towards where Molly was waiting patiently.

'There goes US$350.000,' said Josh mournfully.

'Well I understand that the Mercedes people said to test them to destruction...' said Viktor.

'Why did it take so long? Josh Asked.

Viktor grinned, 'if we had used a normal fuse, we would be in little pieces along with the Merc. What I used is termed a safety fuse which travels at about one foot every 30 seconds. It was invented by and Englishman called William Bickford in 1831, when it was found other fuses were unreliable and caused many deaths.'

'Wish you had told me that before.' said Josh, wiping his brow.

When they returned, Josh looked at his watch, 'it's 15:00 hours,' he said, 'don't forget we have to listen in at 20:00.'

THE SEARCH INTENSIFIES

Chapter 12

Sherepov landed the plane back at Donetsk Airport and travelled back to the General's office. From there he called up the Major who was conducting the search. 'How is it going Major?' 'Well we've narrowed the search as you ordered, but so far we haven't found anything of interest apart from a large cache of drugs in one of the warehouses here.

'The second party found the wreckage of the helicopter and the four on board are all dead, so we've arranged to get their bodies picked up by the ambulance corps.'

'Okay, I want you to send a company over to the spot where I discovered what appeared to be some SAS personnel, it may have been a false alarm, but get them to check the area out.' He gave him coordinates. 'I gave orders for a couple of Su-35's to bomb the area and I'm particularly interested to know if they scored any hits.'

'Okay sir, I'll lead the team myself and call you back as soon as I've any news. Do you have a mobile sir?'

Sherepov said he did and gave the Major his number.

'Remember Major this search must not fail, we must find this man and the documents he is carrying.'

Having given these instructions, Sherepov went back into the map room and laid out the map of the area once again. He took a pencil and drew a ring around the North West area of Donetsk leaving the town itself outside the ring. He then went to a computer, called up Google Earth, and started to scan the area he'd pencilled. To get an accurate picture he worked with a high magnification. It soon became clear that most of the area was barren but he noted about three separate buildings that were isolated. He knew the SAS would normally be operating in the countryside, and he guessed that George Manning would avoid the town area, it being too difficult to escape if cornered. Sherepov resolved to discuss his findings with the Major when he called later in the day.

The company of soldiers led by the Major soon found the area that had been bombed. It was totally devastated, bits of vehicle spread over a large area, but they concluded that only one vehicle was involved and no bodies found. They searched a wider area, about a quarter of a mile in each direction, but found nothing.

The Major decided to report in person to Sherepov, suspecting correctly that the mobile telephone system was not secure. He told the troops to continue their search and took over an hour to get back to Headquarters.

He eventually found Sherepov at his hotel.

'Ah, Major, I thought you were going to call?'

'I thought it best to report in person sir, mobile phones are not safe here.'

Sherepov nodded, 'they are not secure anywhere Major, but no matter let's have drink and discuss what you've found.'

Sherepov ordered a large vodka's and an orange juice. They found a table in a quiet area in the bar.

'Well we found a vehicle or at least pieces of it, all over the gorge, the air force had obviously done a great job, in fact overdone it as there was no sign of any bodies but the devastation was such that is not particularly surprising.'

'Any weapons or pieces of weapons Major?'

'No sir, not as far as I could see, but I've left my people to continue the search and to collect all the debris together so we can analyse it.'

'Hmm, no weapons, no bodies, and the vehicle blown to pieces, what does that tell you Major?'

The Major looked surprised. 'Well...'

'A put-up job Major,' said Sherepov. 'Two vehicles were originally reported by the helicopter crew, not one, which suggests to me that once they knew they had been spotted, they blew up one of the vehicles to lead us off the scent. Now if you were to blow up one of your vehicles, what would you do with your weapons?'

'Yes, I see where you're coming from sir, I'd remove them.'

'Of course, you would, and a bomb from an aircraft; unless a direct hit, would simply throw the vehicle in the air but wouldn't shatter it into bits as you describe, no Major, our enemy is still at large and probably nearer than you think, keep your men searching the gorge area until it's too dark to continue.'

'I've already told them to continue the search sir, but I'll recall them at sunset as you suggest.'

'Good, now let me show you some maps I've printed out from the computer, there are three areas, which I suspect could house our targets, they could be farms or industrial buildings, but all are isolated. What I want you to do is organise your troops into three sections and get them in place near to these buildings by 3 a.m. tomorrow morning and at 4 a.m. precisely we'll carry out a raid on all three.' Sherepov pointed at one of the areas, 'and I'll be with you at this point.' He jabbed his finger on what appeared to be farm buildings.

Molly was sleeping in the back of the Mercedes when Josh quietly opened the door and put his hand over her mouth. She woke up immediately. 'quiet' said Josh, his finger to his lips. 'There's a group of soldiers carrying out a search in the gorge,' he whispered, 'they haven't seen us and as we're very well camouflaged, they may not do so, but just in case here is a sub-machine gun, only fire it if they break in here.'

'How many are there?'

'Appears to be about ten, but there may be others further up, don't worry, we can deal with 'em if we have to, none of them have heavy weapons, so we'll just stay quiet and hope we remain unseen.' With that, he left Molly inside the vehicle and crouched with his sub-machine gun in his hand and a small number of grenades in a pile beside him. Viktor was on top of the Mercedes with the heavy machine gun. He had agreed with Joshua that if it came to a fight, he would stay in position, Josh would drive the vehicle out of cover, and they'd make a run for it while the enemy was still stunned.

As it happened, one soldier started to walk towards them, but was called away by a colleague to study something in the middle of the gorge. After that they disappeared further down the gorge and didn't return. Josh assumed that they had gone down to the bottom and perhaps gone back to their camp as it was getting dark.

'Phew,' said Viktor afterwards, 'that was too close for comfort.' Josh agreed. Molly said that in future she'd stick to hospital wards.

At 20:00 hours Josh stood by on the radio as arranged and Carl came through dead on time. 'You guys Okay?'

'Affirmative,' answered Josh, not wasting radio time with explanations.

'Okay, Desmond and McCauley will meet you at base camp in three hours.'

'Roger out.' Josh closed the transmission, and turned to Viktor and Molly. 'I'll go and meet them at our last location, I'll be able lead them back here. If I set off now, I can ensure that the area is clear and keep a watch, if the ungodly are still there, I can then lead the boss and McCauley off before they reach that point, in fact I may do that anyway.' Josh put on his backpack, which contained some food, water and several grenades, picked up his sub-machine gun and an ugly looking knife and disappeared out of the camouflage.

Having woken from a deep sleep at 19:00 hours, Desmond and McCauley set off from the farm on foot, covering the area in good time considering it was dark and they were not able to use torches. As they were nearing the original base where the vehicles were, Desmond heard a tune being softly whistled which he recognised immediately. He whistled back.

Josh broke cover, 'hi guys, good to see you. I thought I'd head you off as we had to move base, I'll tell you all about it when we get back. We only have one Merc, and that's hidden further down the gorge, so we'll head there directly.' They decided that they'd travel in silence as the night was still and voices could travel.

They all arrived at the new base in the cleft and both Molly and Viktor were relieved to see them. Molly brewed coffee as Josh took up the story. 'We were spotted by a low flying piston engine aircraft, so we immediately moved the vehicles down here, which is actually a better hide,' he explained. 'We were aware that jets had been called in and we heard the bombs dropping.'

'As did we,' confirmed Desmond, 'and we were worried that you guys had been caught unaware.'

'Naw,' answered Josh, 'we've bin trained too well for that, but after the jets had gone, we realised that they would almost certainly send in a posse to see what damage they'd caused, so we took one Merc back and blew it up to give them the idea that they'd done us in.'

'And did they?' asked Desmond,

'Yeah, 'bout a company of Russians comprising about twenty men, they searched the gorge, but didn't see us, which is just as well for them,' grinned Viktor 'as we were ready for 'em.'

John nodded, 'well you did the right thing, well done. Now the plan is to get back to the farm, we were correct in the target incidentally,' he said, 'but it won't be safe for long.

'We're scheduled to call H.Q. at 12:00 midnight tomorrow, now that call will include our coordinates and as it's to be sent in the clear, the ungodly will almost certainly be listening in, so we can expect some unfriendly company pretty quickly. Now it's our job to get George Manning away with his important documents first, after that we can move.'

'Do we drive back?' asked Viktor.

'No Viktor, we'd never make it, and it's essential that none of us is captured as it can never be revealed that George got away, so we intend to blow the farmhouse where we are and pretend that the rescue was a failure.'

'So, what's being sent to pick us up, a Rolls Royce Limo?' laughed Josh.

'Negative, Apache attack helicopters.'

'What,' said Josh, in amazement, 'but they don't...'

'No, normally they don't take passengers, but they'll be fitted with attachments on the fuselage, that will take two each side, now there will be 10 of us altogether and there are going to be six Apaches, so three will land and you have 30 seconds at most to get yourself hitched. So, to make sure we all know exactly what we are going to do, I'll look after George Manning and Sergeant McCauley will look after Molly, the documents will be put in the cabin with the pilot, and once they are strapped on, the chopper will take off.

'The second one to land will take Viktor, Borislav, Josh and Carl and the third will be you McCauley. Ivor, Leond and me, we're not quite sure yet if Leond is going to travel, but that's his call.

'They were going to send in Tornados to cover, but we've advised them against that 'cause there are Su-35's in the area, and the Tornados are not fit for purpose to deal with those guys. The whole mission depends on speed. The Apaches will be flying very low all the way, but they have technology that can deal with that, and as its going to be dark, no moon, it's unlikely that the Su-35's will be in a position to do much about it.'

'One question sir, what happens if one of the Apaches is shot down?'

'Well, there are six on this mission, and three of them won't land, but act as cover and if anyone is taken out, a chopper that's not carrying people will land to take off the pilots and passengers if any, assuming they are still in one piece. They'll then blow up the damaged aircraft so as not to give the Ruskies any advanced technology.'

'If George Manning is successful in getting away, how can you disguise the fact?' asked Viktor.

'We'll leave his personal papers such as his passport in the house along with a couple of the reports that have been taken, and we'll hope that they'll accept that George didn't make it.'

'When we return, it'll be reported to the press that the attempt wasn't successful, and that George was killed in a large explosion before he could reach the aircraft, this type of rescue has been unsuccessful before, so it wouldn't come as a surprise.'

Molly looked worried, 'how fast do these aircraft fly?' she asked.

'About 190 miles per hour,' smiled Desmond, 'but you'll have special cold weather kit to put on including goggles and hood. The flying time will only be about forty minutes, and they'll only go at full speed for the first 50 odd miles until they are out of the danger zone, then they'll slow up unless they have bandits on their tail, which is unlikely.'

'Well it's a new experience I suppose, beats wrapping bandages around people.'

'Let's hope we don't need your services Molly,' said John.

'Right, I've put the rest fully in the picture, so I don't need to go through this again,' John looked at his watch, 'It's almost midnight,' he said, 'time we were getting back. Josh you drive, but keep the noise low and the speed down. I'll sit beside you and about three miles short of our target, we'll stop, and I'll fire up the computer to ensure there's no one else trying to join the party.'

Josh drove carefully back towards the farm and as instructed stopped about three miles short. John fired up his computer and connected to the satellite. He frowned as he studied the area. 'I think they may have company,' he said. 'There's some movement on the southern side of the farm, get them on the radio fast.'

Josh got into the back of the Mercedes and tapped in a code. The farm was on standby and Josh received a code back that they were listening in.

Josh sent a message, 'Bandits at 180 aborting arrival stop. Can you manage, over?'

The message came back. 'We have fail-safe arrangements. Stop, call tomorrow at 10.00. Stop, out.'

The message, sent very quickly meant that even if anyone was listening in, it would have been impossible for them to discover the whereabouts of the transmission.

John was concerned at the soldiers surrounding the farm as he had no knowledge of any fail-safe arrangements, but he realised he had no choice but to accept their assurance.

'Okay Josh,' he said as Josh climbed back into the driving seat. 'Over there,' John pointed, 'there's a large wooded area where the River Samara runs through it, head for that but slowly we don't want to be overheard. He set the coordinates in the GPS system that he'd received from the satellite. It took over twenty minutes to reach the area, and they found a suitable place to hide the Mercedes, where they covered it with the camouflage netting and settled inside to await developments.

THE EXPLOSION

Chapter 13

Friday 22nd May 2015

It happened about 04:15 in the morning. Both Sergeant McCauley and Captain Desmond had been watching the gradual movement of Russian troops surrounding the farm from their vantage point, completed very professionally and in almost total silence.

Kieran was getting particularly restive, he turned to John, 'they are only about 20 men with relatively light arms. Don't you think we should intervene?'

John shook his head, 'the guys down there are aware of the situation, we'll wait to see what happens, if we think they can't manage, we'll intervene. Just be patient McCauley.'

'I'm not happy with that decision sir.'

'Okay Sergeant if we intervene now, we don't know where our guys are, we could be shooting each other, and as the Russians are well spread out, we would be bound to take casualties. We stay put until the situation is clearer,' said John finally.

Suddenly there was mayhem; one of the Russians drove a light armoured vehicle through the double gates at speed followed by a dozen soldiers firing their sub-machine guns wildly. There appeared to be no response. The remainder of the troops closed in and it was apparent that they were searching the property. Most were now inside the fortified area, although a couple of soldiers were outside the gates smoking cigarettes. There appeared to be a civilian in the centre giving the orders and Desmond saw several items including a sub-machine gun brought out and shown to the civilian.

Suddenly there was a huge explosion, so violent that both John and Kieran felt the whoosh of the after-shock.

'Jesus, what the hell was that?'

'I think our friend Carl has been at work,' answered John, 'but I didn't see any of them leave.' He looked puzzled.

'Nor me,' said Kieran, 'and we've bin here most of the night.'

Soon they were aware of the sound of ambulances with their distinctive bells and other vehicles racing to the spot, one of soldiers outside the gates was staggering around; the other was lying some distance away. The area filled with vehicles, and a General's car appeared, the occupant getting out and walking inside the compound. As he did so, there was another explosion, which caught the first medics to arrive, they saw one of the large ambulances rise high into the air and crash down on top of another.

Molly, Josh and Viktor, who couldn't believe their eyes, joined John and Kieran. 'What happened?' asked Molly.

John smiled, 'I guess the bandits got a little too curious. I must admit the size of the first explosion surprised me, as Carl didn't have any explosives with him, we have them all here, at least those that were left after blowing up the other Merc. I can only think that Ivor had previously laid the ground in case they should be attacked, but how they did it, I've no idea.'

'The problem we have,' said Kieran, 'is that the enemy is not going to be very happy, they'll be scouring the countryside for revenge, and we'll be right in their path. If the guy who got out of the General's car was the General, I saw flying through the air, then the bandits are going to be really pissed off.'

'Yes, you're right Kieran, but we haven't finished our job yet. 1. We have to find out where our guys are holed up, and get them out, and 2. We have to sit tight somewhere until the cavalry come for us, so, anyone any bright ideas?'

'Yes, I have,' said Molly. Everyone looked at her in surprise.

'Go on Molly,' said John.

'I've my nurses' outfit in the vehicle, I suggest I change, and walk down to what's left of the farm. If I'm stopped then I can say that I've been sent to see if there are any more casualties.'

'You'll speak to them in English of course?' Kieran sneered.

'Net. Ya budu goverit na russkom yazke.'

Kieran opened his mouth. 'What?' he exclaimed.

Viktor translated, 'she said "no, she'd speak in Russian".' he grinned.

John smiled, 'we didn't know you spoke the language, Molly.'

'I took it as my first language at school, that's why I volunteered for this job.'

'What good do you think you might do down there?' asked Viktor.

'Well I can look around to see if there's any clue as to where our friends have gone, and I may be able to find out if any of them were caught in the explosion.'

'Okay,' said John, 'thank you Molly, I appreciate your offer, and I may take you up on it later, but right now we have other problems to deal with and if we split our forces even more then we may have real problems getting everyone together in time. What we need to do is to assess whether we will be safe here until 10:00 hours when we agreed to contact Ivor.

'We're in a fairly remote part, and we're well camouflaged, we have fast wheels if we need to move quickly. For you to walk from here over open ground wouldn't only look strange, but would be considered very odd indeed, particularly if you were in a nurse's uniform. I suggest we stay here until at least 10:00, and take a view then. In the meantime, let's look at other alternatives as to what we might do in certain circumstances, not forgetting our prime reason for being here, and that's to get George and his documents back to Kiev.'

That's what they did, and while they could see quite a lot of movement down on the farm, there didn't appear to be any immediate indication of a broader search.

At 10:00, Josh opened the wireless connection and tapped in the code.

'Read you loud & clear,' was the answer.

'Is everything OK?'

'Yes'.

'ETA collection and position?'

'Call 23.00, out.'

Again, the transmission was very short and very much to the point. John got his team together once again. 'Okay guys, that tells me that they are close by, as originally the pick-up was at midnight. Therefore, they are giving us an hour to get to them and organise ourselves. they have indicated that everything is okay...'

'We are assuming that they have not been captured and someone else is...'

'No' said Josh, 'that was definitely Carl, I can tell by his "signature" and in any case he would have made a deliberate mistake if he was under duress.'

'Alright.' said John. 'Question, are we safe to stay here?'

'I don't think so boss,' said Kieran, 'if there was a general search, and its highly likely there will be one, then we would have to break cover in daylight, and we'd be run down from the air within a few minutes.'

'But if we break cover now, it could have same result,' argued Viktor.'

'Okay,' said John, 'we're on high ground, so we can see a good fifteen miles or more to the east and south. There's another large wooded area to the north east which is about ten miles long, we could head for that if we had a problem, it's only about half a mile away, which we could cover in no time at all in the Mercedes. Once in there we could lose ourselves.'

'As the tail of that wood is nearer to the farm, wouldn't it be better to make for there now?' Kieran was eager to move.

'Why? we don't know where the others are, and as they don't have enough transport to move; at least so far as we know, we're going to have to move ourselves to where they indicate,' answered John.

'It may be,' said Molly 'that they'll assume that everyone was killed in the explosion.'

'Yeah, and pigs may fly,' answered Kieran.

'Okay guys, I suggest we get some sleep and we'll take a view tomorrow,' said John, 'I'll take the first watch. We'll do two hours each, Kieran you can relieve me.'

Kieran proved to be right, as around midday several truckloads of soldiers arrived at the farm, they fanned out in a north westerly direction, straight towards where they were hiding. They had dogs and there were two helicopters joining the search.

'Fuck,' said Kieran, 'now we're for it.'

'Okay,' said John, 'here's what we'll do. We'll drive up the north west of the wood to the northern end, then when the choppers are on their southern patrol, we'll make a run for it across to the long wood north east, Viktor and Kieran you'll man the stinger and the heavy machine gun. If they catch us up, they'll get a dousing. At 60 M.P.H. we should cover that ground in less than 3 minutes but it looks flat so we may do better. Once there we'll travel north under the cover of the wood, if we're seen they won't be able to get their jets out in time. When we reach the top, we can swing right on to the T404 and then head south, that's if we haven't been spotted. They'll know that we're well armed, so they'll move with caution. If we find that they are going in a different direction we can hold out at the top of the wood and then move when we get instructions.'

They executed the manoeuvre perfectly and reached the second wood without being seen, they then travelled up a track on the east side of the wood preparing to pull in under cover should they be spotted. When they reached the top, they discovered that the search party had turned west and were heading towards the original gorge.

At 23:00 hours, Josh fired up his radio and called the special code, it was answered immediately. Carl sent the GPS coordinates. He gave it to them in letters rather than numbers, N-DHOGHEB E-CGFFGIDG and it took Josh a few moments to realise what he'd done; he converted them into numbers. 'Ok, got it, let's go.'

He gunned the engine, they moved across to the T404, and the GPS took them south. The road was very quiet, so they had no problems.

'It's taking us back to the farm,' said Viktor.

Sure enough, just before the farm they turned left and up a rough track, then after about quarter of a mile right on to the middle of a field.

There appeared to be no one about. 'I don't like the look of this,' said McCauley, looking around. Just then there was a tap on the window, it was Carl. 'Hey Carl how are ...'

'Later,' he said. 'Drive straight on and in a hundred yards you'll come to Ivor and Leond by what appears to be a large hole in the ground, drive straight in and down the slope stopping at the bottom.'

Josh did so, he noticed in his mirror Carl running behind them and the camouflaged cover closing above him.

As soon as the overhead door closed, a dim light went on showing a complex of doors in front of them. They all climbed out of the Mercedes and were led through one of the doors into a large cavernous area where hugs were exchanged all round. There was a large table in the centre with hot coffee brewed on a side table on a primus stove.

John sat down with Ivor, George and Carl while the others went to get ready for the expected exit as soon as the aircraft arrived.

Josh had been asked to listen out on the radio, as they'd had a short message indicating that the aircraft would be late, but would transmit the code "CALLING CARD" three times when ten minutes away. They requested that a flare be sent up when they could be heard approaching.

John received his coffee and sipped it gratefully. 'What happened?' he asked. 'We saw the explosion from the wood about three miles away and were concerned that you guys had been caught in it.'

Ivor grinned, 'No, we were advised by a friend who works in the General's office that they were on their way. We were going to blow the place up anyway, but we thought it better to await their arrival before doing so. Carl gave us a hand with the final touches because we had quite a lot of ammunition stacked down here, and he wired it all in for us.'

'But how did you get out?' asked John.

'Ah, when my family bought the property many years ago, they discovered a large cave underneath the field, where we are now in fact. They came across a bricked-up entrance from the basement under the farm, so we assume it must have been a fortified farm way back in history with a back-door escape. We broke down the wall put in a steel door instead and disguised it by placing a heavy steel cupboard in front that could only be moved by an electrical piece of equipment normally used to open a car. No one searching the place could move it without the electronic key.

'We then constructed an entrance at the other end of the cave, with a large steel pad powered by hydraulic rams and run by high-powered batteries, which opens to allow a vehicle in. The internal concrete slope was constructed at the same time.

'We then built in various rooms including sleeping quarters, to be self-sufficient. The sewerage is simply connected to the mains as is the water. There are so many leaks in the public water system here that no one has noticed, not that we use a lot of course.'

'The entrance from the farm will be covered in rubble now of course but we'll put in an extra concrete wall from this side just in case they clear the rubble away and it's exposed.'

'What about air?' George asked.

'Well, there must be an outlet somewhere as the air in here is fresh, but we've never found it.' He grinned, 'the beauty of it is that we could keep a small army down here unnoticed, and in fact my guys are staying here as I've some ideas to put to your people in Kiev.'

'You mean your guys,' said John.

'No, Kiev is as leaky as hell; this place has to remain secret, which it certainly wouldn't do if we informed the government there about its whereabouts. But it may be useful for the CIA or Special Forces like you.'

George frowned, 'but surely the tyre tracks from the Mercedes would lead the ungodly to this place?'

'No, we don't bring many vehicles down here for a start, but when we do, we put down a special thick carpet like stuff, and then remove it afterwards. We did this for the Mercedes, as that could be quite a useful bit of kit along with all the other stuff you brought with you.'

Josh burst into the room, '10 minutes; we need to get upside now.' John looked at his date watch it was 01:00 hours Saturday 23rd May 2015.

There was a flurry of activity and the rear entrance rose for the second time that evening. Leond had decided to stay with the others, so Ivor went around each of his men giving them a hug and promising to return soon. Then those leaving walked out into the cold night air and as soon as everyone one was outside, the pad covering the cave was silently closed.

John could see several trucks in the distance travelling towards the farm and he pointed this out to Kieran. 'We need to move away from this point,' said Ivor, 'if those trucks are what I think they are, they must have intercepted our message earlier, and it's important that the cave is not compromised.' They all ran to the other end of the field and as they did so Kieran was the first to hear the approaching aircraft. He put a flare into the flare gun and fired. The whole area was bathed in light and within two minutes the first aircraft was hovering close to the ground, the other two following almost immediately afterwards. One stayed in the air, which was going to be the leader out, but the other two turned towards the trucks that were now less than a mile away.

As planned, three of the helicopters now landed and the warm clothing thrown down from the cabins, John helped George into his and Kieran helped Molly, both ensured that George and Molly were fastened securely and after giving the pilot George's documents he gave the thumbs up sign to the pilot who immediately took off. He headed west following the lead aircraft at about 50 feet avoiding the area of the trucks. The next aircraft took Viktor, Carl, Josh and Borislav and the final Apache took Ivor, John, and Kieran.

To prevent anyone from the trucks firing a ground to air missile at the fast disappearing Apaches, the two left as sentries, fired off two hellfire missiles at each of the trucks and there were huge explosions as they hit home. The pilot of the rear Apache saw soldiers thrown in the air with others running away from the trucks, some of them on fire.

The Apaches turned and followed their colleagues as rear defenders. They only once noted some fire from the ground, but it was wild and nobody was hit.

George said afterwards that it was the ride of his life, strapped to the outside of the machine the wind ripped at his clothing and at one stage he thought the straps holding him on the fuselage would break with the strain, but after about fifteen minutes the aircraft slowed and the trip was relatively pleasant.

As soon as they arrived, George, was released from the Apache and bundled into a waiting Jet Ranger along with his documents, the aircraft taking off heading west towards Kiev. George had not removed his warm clothing and found himself sweating until he eventually managed to get out of the garments. It was too noisy to talk to the pilots in front, so he attempted to sleep, but that didn't work either. He looked out of the window at the lights below as they sped further west. It took almost an hour to reach the destination, and George was helped out of the aircraft and taken straight towards a car with blacked out windows in the rear waiting on the tarmac. As he was steered towards it, two US Marines took the documents from him and sat either side of him while the driver moved at some speed out of the military airbase. George noticed that there were two more cars accompanying them, one in front and one behind. Someone was taking no chances he thought.

It took twenty minutes to reach the American Embassy, and as they reached the gates, they were opened immediately and the cars driven into the fortified compound. George noticed that the area was completely closed off to any outside observers. A marine opened the rear door of the car and saluted George as he climbed out. In front of him standing in the main entrance was Bill Cummins with a huge smile on his face. He shook George's hand vigorously, 'well done, very well done, please come inside.' George followed him in to the lobby area and one of the marines brought in the package and gave it to Bill.

He turned to George, 'Come on up to my office George, I guess you could do with a strong drink?' he raised his eyebrows as they took the elevator to the top floor.

Once in the Ambassador's office, George received a large Brandy as he melted into a comfortable chair. He suddenly felt very tired, as the adrenalin in his body subsided.

Bill Cummins sat down opposite him. 'We've arranged for you to sleep here tonight George, we can get together tomorrow, when you're ready,' he said hastily recognising George's tired looking face.

George suddenly realised that he had left his case behind in the farm and that he had no change of clothing, not even a toothbrush. He told the Ambassador.

He laughed, 'don't worry George, you'll find everything that's necessary in your room, and we can sort the rest out when we talk tomorrow.'

'One thing more,' said George, 'I need to call my wife.'

Bill Cummins nodded, 'all in good time George, don't worry, she's in good hands in the CIA village in Florida, and she's aware of the situation.'

George looked alarmed, 'but that's usually the place they take families who've lost their husbands,' he exclaimed, now worried.

'Yes, it is, but I'm afraid we had to kill you off, otherwise the Russians would have known that we had the package, and it would have lost a lot of its value. Be very sure though that your wife knows that you're okay and she'll be told that you are now safe here in Kiev. What we intend to do is to have a debriefing session with you and then send you to Washington in a military aircraft to hand over the package to the people in Langley, Jim Wallace will be going with you. As soon as you've finished there, you'll be flown down to Florida to spend some time with your family and then back to Washington where you'll become involved on the planning front, but we'll discuss all that tomorrow.'

SHEREPOV QUESTIONS

Chapter 14

After the explosion at the farm, the medics on the scene found Sherepov face down in the dirt, and along with many others, he was taken to the military hospital. At first, because he was in civilian clothes, it was considered that he might be one of the enemies, later he was recognised by the Major who identified those that had been killed and those who had survived, Sherepov was immediately given priority and moved to a private room. His injuries were not as bad as originally thought. He'd been outside the buildings when the explosion happened and this saved him from being seriously injured. He had a piece of wood that had gone through his shin and a broken arm, but it was a clean break, and a punctured eardrum. By the fourth day Sherepov had discharged himself from the hospital, he'd asked the Major to pick him up and take him to the farm. There was basically nothing left, all the buildings destroyed, leaving a huge pile of rubble.

As he limped into the centre of the area, he asked, 'Were all the soldiers identified Major?'

'So far sir, we have a total of 12 dead 2 very seriously injured, three still in hospital and one man who appears to have escaped with very minor injuries.'

'The General was one of those killed I understand.'

'Yes sir.'

'So how many soldiers were there in total?'

'21 Sir, 22 including the General and 23 including you.'

'So, if my mathematics are right, we have four people missing.'

'Yes sir, as you can see, we are still digging through the rubble, but it's highly unlikely that we'll find anyone alive.'

Sherepov nodded, 'I understand that, but have all the people that we've found been definitely identified?'

'Yes sir.'

'So, where is the mysterious George Manning who the Americans claim was killed in the explosion?'

The Major shrugged, 'his body may well be under this lot,' he pointed to the rubble.

'Yes, he may be, but don't you find it strange that we've not found anyone who may have been in the farm at the time?'

'Not necessarily sir, the farm has been deserted for some time.'

'Hmm, now tell me about the incursion of helicopters on the night after the explosion.'

'We were reacting to a message we picked up giving coordinates, but it was from the field at the back of the farm, not from the farm itself.

'By the time we got near to the area the helicopters were moving away, we assume they came in on a rescue mission, but seeing the farm destroyed, they simply returned. They did fire some missiles at our trucks causing casualties, but they were in and out very quickly.'

'Has the area been thoroughly searched?'

'Yes sir, as I've said, the coordinates were not from the farm itself, as the choppers couldn't have landed there.'

'What sort of helicopters were they?'

'According to one of the senior non-commissioned officers they were Apaches.'

'Apaches, they don't carry passengers.'

'No sir, we assume that there must have been a transport machine somewhere behind, but when it found there were no survivors, it probably turned around. The Apaches would have been for protection only.'

'Hmm, I wonder. Look major, I want this area completely cleaned out and all bodies found and identified, you have two days, so before I return to Moscow you need to get some diggers in here.'

The Major saluted, 'Yes sir, I'll get to work on that immediately.'

Sherepov told his driver to take him to the military HQ where he found a secure phone in the ex-General's office. He dialled a number.

'American Ambassador.'

'Good morning Ambassador,'

'Yes, Sherepov, I hear you were injured.'

'Only slightly, but I've a quick question.'

'Yes?'

'Have you had any indication from your end that George Manning escaped?'

'No, I've been informed of his death and his wife has been withdrawn back to the States.'

'Did you see her before she went?'

'No, it's normal when this sort of thing happens, the CIA move the families out very quickly.'

'No one reported to you of a distraught wife?'

'No, but none of my people dealt with the matter. Why Sherepov, are you unsure of his demise?'

'Hmm, just a feeling.'

'Well, keep me informed and if I hear anything from this end, I'll be in touch.'

It was only 24 hours later that the Major reported.

'All the missing bodies have been accounted for, sir.'

'George Manning?'

'No sir, but it's possible that he was blown to pieces as there was quite a lot of blood and gore down there.'

'But why should Manning be the only one to be blown to pieces Major?' Sherepov shook his head, 'no, either he escaped to Kiev, which seems unlikely as the transport helicopter wasn't seen, or he's still here, in which case you should continue your searches.'

THE DE BRIEFING

Chapter 15

Saturday 23rd May

The next morning, despite his experience the day before, George was up quite early and at 08:00 he was served breakfast in his room. The maid being surprised that he was up and dressed. There was a note on his tray stating that there was a meeting starting at 09:00 but it would be understood if he didn't come in until later in the morning.

It was quite a surprise to Bill Cummins that George was the first in the meeting room.

'George, we didn't expect you to drag yourself up quite so early,' Bill smiled and shook his hand.

George had a pad in front of him where his name was printed. 'Looking at the agenda, I wouldn't have missed this for anything,' he laughed. 'I see the report of my death is the first subject.'

Gradually the other invited members filed in to the room and when everyone was present, Bill Cummins started the introductions. 'Good morning Gentlemen, thank you all for coming. Most of you know each other; nevertheless, I'll go through the introductions of all the people sitting round the table. On my right Jim Wallace, Head of CIA Station Ukraine, George Manning, Deputy Head of CIA Moscow, Peter Lienster Deputy Head of CIA, Ukraine and Malcolm Saunders, Deputy American Ambassador. On my left James Winston-Jones, British Ambassador to Ukraine, Douglas Armitage of MI6, Colonel Watson Commanding officer of the British Forces Training Team and finally at the bottom of the table Mrs. Shaw, my personal secretary who will take notes.

'Before reading out the agenda, I would personally like to thank the British contingent for their help and support, as without them we couldn't have pulled this off. Secondly I would like to thank George Manning here for the huge risks he took in getting this very important information to us.' Everyone round the table clapped. 'I would also like to say how sorry we are that our Head of CIA Station Mary Clancy gave up her life for this information, which gives me an extra impetus to ensure it is fully used to deal with the perpetrators of her murder.'

Just then, the coffee and biscuits came in and were distributed around the table.

Bill Cummins made sure everyone had a chance to get sugar or milk as they required before continuing.

'Now gentlemen the agenda:

1. The Press Release
1. The List of Assassinations
2. The Russian policy document for aggression
    a. The Question of the American Ambassador to Moscow.
3. The next move
4. Any other business.

'It is with great regret that we have to announce the death of George Manning,' he smiled, 'it is necessary as you'll see.'

'This is the press release we intend to put out:

on 16th May 2015 persons unknown murdered the Head of our Political Section in Moscow. It is also with great regret that we announce that the Deputy Head of the Political department also lost his life when investigating certain matters in the Ukraine. Our forces, sent in to extract him from Donetsk, found that he had been killed in a large explosion in a building north west of that city. Unfortunately, important documents he was carrying were also destroyed in the explosion.

'That's it gentlemen, we couldn't of course mention the British part in this as that would cause embarrassment to their government, I understand that our President is giving each member of the party a special medal, but this will not be publicised.

'Now to get to the meat of the matter we've received what appear to be original documents of signed orders by the President of Russia regarding the assassination of the following people.

'The latest being Boris Nemtsov a physicist and politician who was due to give evidence against the Russian government regarding the Ukraine situation, and two days before a peace rally which he'd organised. Nemtsov was aware that his life was in danger but he spoke to an old friend Yevgenia Albats, editor of the New Times Magazine two weeks before the murder.

'He said he thought the hierarchy wouldn't have him killed because he was a former member of the Russian Government, and a vice premier, so the President wouldn't want to set a precedent because the power in Russia may change and the current President wouldn't want to encourage the same treatment.'

'Obviously Nemtsov seriously underestimated the way the state now does their business,' said Jim Wallace.

Bill nodded, 'a fatal mistake, to be sure.

'The following list is of people who have been assassinated since 1998 during Putin's reign. The comments, after the names included by our research department working through the night, were extracted from La Russophobe, which is incidentally published on the World Wide Web.

'**November 1998** Less than four months after Putin takes over at the KGB, opposition Duma Deputy Galina Starovoitova, the most prominent pro-democracy Kremlin critic in the nation, is murdered at her apartment building in St. Petersburg. Four months afterwards, Putin will play a key role in silencing the Russian Attorney General, Yury Skuratov, who was investigating high-level corruption in the Kremlin, by airing an illicit sex video involving Skuratov on national TV. Four months after the dust settles in the Skuratov affair, Putin became Prime Minister.

'**April 2003** Sergei Yushenkov, co-chairman of the Liberal Russia political party, is gunned down at the entrance of his Moscow apartment block.

'Yushenkov had been serving as the vice chair of the group known as the "Kovalev Commission" which was formed to informally investigate charges that Putin's KGB had planted the Pechatniki and Kashirskoye apartment bombs to whip up support for Putin's war in Chechnya after the formal legislative investigation turned out to be impossible.

'Another member of the Commission, Yuri Shchekochikhin perished of poisoning, a third severely beaten by thugs, and two other members lost their seats in the Duma.

'The Commission's lawyer, Mikhail Trepashkin was jailed after a secret trial on espionage charges. Today, virtually none of the members of the Commission are left.

'**July 2003** Yuri Shchekochikhin, a vocal opposition journalist and member of the

Russian Duma and the Kovalev Commission, suddenly contracted a mysterious illness. Witnesses reported: "He complained about fatigue, and red blotches began to appear on his skin.

'His internal organs began collapsing one by one. Then he lost almost all his hair." One of Shchekochikhin's last newspaper articles before his death was entitled *"Are we Russia or KGB of Soviet Union?"*

'In it, he described such issues as the refusal of the FSB to explain to the Russian Parliament what poison gas was infiltrated during the Moscow theatre hostage crisis, and the work of secret services from the former Soviet republic of Turkmenistan, which operated with impunity in Moscow against Russian citizens of Turkoman origin.

'According to Wikipedia: "He also tried to investigate the Three Whales Corruption Scandal and criminal activities of FSB officers related to money laundering through the Bank of New York and illegal actions of Yevgeny Adamov, a former Russian Minister of Nuclear Energy."

'This case was under the personal control of Putin. In June of 2003, Shchekochikhin contacted the FBI and got an American visa to discuss the case with US authorities.

'However, he never made it to the USA because of his sudden death on July 3rd. The Russian authorities refused to allow an autopsy, but according to Wikipedia his relatives "managed to send a specimen of his skin to London. A tentative diagnosis was made of poisoning with thallium" (a poison commonly used by the KGB, at first suspected in the Litvinenko death).

'**June 2004** Nikolai Girenko, a prominent human rights defender, Professor of Ethnology and expert on racism and discrimination in the Russian Federation is shot dead in his home in St Petersburg. Girenko's work has been crucial in ensuring that racially motivated assaults are classified as hate crimes, rather than mere hooliganism, and therefore warrant harsher sentences — as well as appearing as black marks on Russia's public record.

'**July 2004** Paul Klebnikov, editor of the Russian edition *Forbes* magazine, is shot and killed in Moscow.

'*Forbes* has reported that at the time of his death, Paul was believed to have been investigating a complex web of money laundering involving a Chechen reconstruction fund, reaching into the centres of power in the Kremlin and involving elements of organised crime and the FSB. (the former KGB).

'**September 2006** Andrei Kozlov, First Deputy Chairman of Russia's Central Bank, who strove to stamp out money laundering (basically acting on analyses like that of reporter Klebnikov), the highest-ranking reformer in Russia, is shot and killed in Moscow. Many media reports classify Kozlov's killing as "an impudent challenge to all Russian authorities" and warn that "failure to apprehend the killers would send a signal to others that intimidation of government officials is once again an option."

'Less considered is the possibility that Kozlov, like Klebnikov, was on the trail of corruption that would have led into the Kremlin itself, which then lashed out at him pre-emptively assuming he could not be bought.

'**October 2006** Anna Politkovskaya, author of countless books and articles exposing Russian human rights violations in Chechnya and attacking Vladimir Putin as a dictator, is shot and killed at her home in Moscow.

'In her book *Putin's Russia*, Politkovskaya had written: "I've wondered a great deal why I've so got it in for Putin. What is it that makes me dislike him so much as to feel moved to write a book about him? I'm not one of his political opponents or rivals, just a woman living in Russia.

"'Quite simply, I am a 45-year-old Muscovite who observed the Soviet Union at its most disgraceful in the 1970s and '80s. I really don't want to find myself back there again." Analysts begin to talk openly of Kremlin complicity in the ongoing string of attacks.

'*Washington Post* columnist Anne Applebaum writes: "Local businessmen had no motivation to kill her — but officials of the army, the police and even the Kremlin did. Whereas local thieves might have tried to cover their tracks, Politkovskaya's assassin, like so many Russian assassins, didn't seem to fear the law."

'There are jitters already: A few hours after news of Politkovskaya's death became public, a worried friend sent a link to an eerie Russian Web site that displays photographs of "enemies of the people" — all Russian journalists and human rights activists, some quite well known.

'Above the pictures are each person's birth date and a blank space where, it is implied, the dates of their deaths will soon be marked. "That sort of thing will make many, and probably most, Russians think twice before criticising the Kremlin about anything".

'**November 2006** Alexander Litvinenko, KGB defector and author of the book *Blowing up Russia*, which accuses the Kremlin of masterminding the Pechatniki and Kashirskoye bombings in order to blame Chechen terrorists and whip up support for an invasion of Chechnya (which shortly followed), is fatally poisoned by radioactive Polonium obtained from Russian sources. Litivinenko had given sensational testimony to the Kovalev Commission and warned Sergei Yushenkov that he was a KGB target.

In his last days Litvinenko himself, as well as other KGB defectors, including Oleg Kalugin, Yuri Shvets and Mikhail Trepashkin (who allegedly actually warned Litvinenko that he had been targeted before the hit took place) directly blamed the Kremlin for ordering the poisoning.

'Recent press reports indicate that British investigators have come to the same conclusion.

'With Litvinenko out of the picture, the only member of the Kovalev Commission left unscathed is its 77-year-old namesake chairman, dissident Sergei Kovalev — who has grown notably silent.

'**March 2007** on Sunday February 25th, the American TV news magazine *Dateline NBC* aired a report on the killing of Litvinenko. MSNBC also carried a report. The reports confirmed that British authorities believe Litvinenko perished in a "state-sponsored" assassination.

'In the opening of the broadcast, *Dateline* highlighted the analysis of a senior British reporter and a senior American expert on Russia who knew Litvinenko well. Here's an excerpt from the MSNBC report:

'Daniel McGrory, a senior correspondent for *The Times of London*, has reported many of the developments in the Litvinenko investigation. He said the police were stuck between a rock and a hard place. "While they claim, and the Prime Minister, Tony Blair, has claimed nothing will be allowed to get in the way of the police investigation, the reality is the police are perfectly aware of the diplomatic fallout of this story,"

'McGrory said. "Let's be frank about this: The United States needs a good relationship with Russia, and so does Europe," said Paul M. Joyal, a friend of Litvinenko's with deep ties as a consultant in Russia and the former Soviet states.

'Noting that Russia controls a significant segment of the world gas market, Joyal said: "This is a very important country. But how can you have an important relationship with a country that could be involved in activities such as this? It's a great dilemma."

'Five days before the broadcast aired, shortly after he was interviewed for it, McGrory was dead. His obituary reads "found dead at his home on February 20, 2007, aged 54." Five days after the broadcast aired, Joyal was lying in a hospital bed after having been shot for no apparent reason, ostensibly the victim of a crazed random street crime.

'He was returning home after having dinner with KGB defector Oleg Kalugin, and had been an aggressive advocate for Georgian independence from Russian influence. The attack remains unsolved.

'**January 2009** On January 19, 2009, Russian human rights attorney Stanslav Markelov was shot in the back of the head with a silenced pistol.

'It happened as he left a press conference at which he announced his intention to sue the Russian government for its early release of the Col. Yuri Budanov, who murdered his 18-year-old client in Chechnya five years earlier. Also, shot and killed was Anastasia Barburova, a young journalism student who was working for Novaya Gazeta and who had studied under Anna Politkovskaya, reporting on the Budanov proceedings.

'**July 2009** On July 14, 2009, leading Russian human rights journalist and activist

Natalia Estemirova, a single mother of a teenage daughter, was abducted in front of her home in Grozny, Chechnya, spirited across the border into Ingushetia, shot and dumped in a roadside gutter.

'Viewed as the successor to Anna Politkovskaya and by far the most prominent living critic of Chechen strongman Ramzan Kadyrov, who had repeatedly threatened her life, Estemirova was a member of the "Memorial" human rights NGO and a steadfast defender of human rights in Chechnya.

'Most recently, she had been reporting on the barbaric practice of the government in burning down the homes of rebel activists, often with women and children locked inside.

'February 2015 Boris Nemtsov was shot and killed just before midnight in February. He was shot several times in the back as he was crossing the Bolshoy Moskvoresky Bridge in Moscow, close to the Kremlin walls and the Red Square.

'Russian journalist Kseniya Sobchak said that Nemtsov was preparing a report proving the presence of Russian military in eastern Ukraine despite its heated denial from senior sources in Moscow.

'A posthumous report in the New York Times stated that Nemtsov, two weeks before his murder, had met with an old friend to discuss the latest research into what he said was dissembling and misdeeds in the Kremlin.

'The friend, Yevgenia Albats, editor of New Times magazine, said that Nemtsov planned to call the report "Putin and the War", because it focused on Russia's role in the Ukraine conflict. Albats commented on her fear for Nemtsov's life due to this specific revealing project of his.'

Bill Cummins looked up from reading the list along with the comments. 'You will appreciate that these are only the higher profile victims, there have many more murders and many more put in prison under some flimsy and doubtful evidence.

'Now gentlemen I move to a summary of the detailed plan which has been hatched up by the Kremlin spelling out their future strategy.

He began reading the Preamble:

'REPORT ON RUSSIA'S FUTURE

'Democracy is not the answer for Russia. It doesn't work and you only have to look at the weakness of the western democracies to see why. The problem is not just giving the masses too much freedom but all politicians in the western world vie with each other to give more to the electorate than the country can afford. People are inherently greedy, they are given their freedom but they want more from the state without the state controlling them or very often without them putting any more effort into making the State successful. This means that western democracies borrow more to placate their electorate, by borrowing more and giving more weakens the state.

'China has shown the way by having a strong leadership control of the press, no human rights and a strong military that not only defends but also controls the indigenous. If we're not careful they are the ones that will take over the world, not because they have a strong economy, but because they control their electorate absolutely. Russia must do the same as China; increase the borders, increase the population and continue to weaken the resolve of the west, a polyglot of disfranchised people who cannot agree on anything.

'It is said that the USA is strong because of its economy, but it is squandering its reserves on ungrateful and perfidious peoples across the world that more and more see it as a bully. It is supported deliberately by China who as the banker sees it as the wayward customer, who they are prepared to loan money to while they steal their secret technology. Their plan is to get them used to spending more and more and then cut them off.

'Only the strong will survive the future and it is our view that we should work to take advantage of the western democracies; feed their desires, slowly take over their influence areas and threaten their allies and then strike at their heart; which is their greed. We are already seeing situations where states within states want more control, we should foster them.

'Scotland is a good example of this where they want to cancel Britain's nuclear armaments. Excellent, that will leave Britain defenceless and because of the greed of that nation's people with the ever-increasing spending on free health and welfare, they will continue to spend less on defence and more importantly the technology that supports it.

We will use our energy surplus to control those countries in Europe that are already dependent on our gas, and oil, utilise our considerable expertise in cyber warfare which will threaten the west's dependence on smart machinery and carry out fake news to destabilise countries with Soviet citizens such as those in the Baltic States, and interfere through financing greedy businessmen and politicians to weaken the democratic systems.

'Due to our influence, we already see this happening in NATO where most countries spend less than half of their commitment on defence despite their treaties, they know that the USA cannot afford to see them invaded, but the USA will become much weaker in the future as strong political unions like Russia and China take over.

'These advanced countries are already selling their souls to the devil in the form of China. Why are they doing so? Because they perceive they make more money; they do not look into the future and consider that China will willingly take their technology and their expertise and then bleed them dry.

'They will then be glad to join a strong and united State like Russia. We should work to make Russia the most powerful country in the world and that will be achieved by harnessing Europe for a start. We know China is our real eventual enemy and so we need to be strong, for that it is where the clash of the titans will be fought for complete world authority.

'Hitler had the right idea, but he chose the wrong enemy. He should have finished Britain off to isolate the United States and continued his thrust south and east after having taken Crete, the Middle East was ripe for expansion.

'His view on anti-Semitism was also correct the Jews are a subversive in our society; we need to further the Slav cause and we'll not make the same mistakes as he did. Remember how Europe crumbled in Word War 2, and how quickly the people were subjugated.

'Hitler acted too quickly, if he had been a little subtler and like Russia used "maskirovka", (*stealth in English*), he would have been able to attack Russia from the west and the south and would have probably persuaded the Japanese to attack us from the south and east. In those days, many countries would have considered him a liberator.'

A written report for the politburo
Dated August 2014.

Bill Cummins looked up taking a glass of water as he did so.

'Well gentleman that was a preamble of a report that was sent to the President in August last year, we have no knowledge of it actually reaching the Politburo. We know however, that anti-Semitism is rising in Russia and may become a problem for not only the Jewish people there but also anyone who is not of Slav origin.

'We've looked at the strategy report for 2015 – 2020. I've asked my people to give a summary of this quite large report as it needs some real in-depth study, but what they have extracted will give you an idea of where they are going.

'Because my mouth is a bit dry, I've asked Mrs. Shaw to read from this Report.'

Mrs. Shaw assembled the sheets in front her. She looked up and smiled, adjusting her glasses as she started to read.

'This report starts with what has been achieved so far and then goes into detail of where Russia goes from here. As an historian, I'm interested in the way the plan is laid out along with a map showing where Russia intends to spread its influence. Hitler did something very similar in 1937, unfortunately for him we received a copy from a German official working in their cryptology section, which his brother headed. The Poles turned this fellow by offering cash for secrets and then passed the documentation over to us.

'This Russian document mentions the virtual annexation of Chechnya, the annexation of part of Georgia Abkhazia and South Ossetia. With the Crimea annexed, now they are establishing an independent state in east Ukraine. These incursions have been more of a test of USA and European resolve than any serious attempt at increasing their land borders. NATO and the west have been particularly reticent to become involved despite the rhetoric coming out of the UK, France and USA.

'We know that only four countries within the 28 members of NATO are actually meeting their defence treaties and they are UK, USA, Greece and Lithuania. They are supposed to reach 2 percent of GDP but most are in fact cutting their expenditures perhaps even including the UK. It is reported that they will all be under the two percent figure in 2016.

'Russia is increasing its military expenditure to over four percent of GDP and at the same time increasing their expenditure on bringing their nuclear forces up to date.' Mrs. Shaw looked up, 'we should remember that Russia still has more nuclear weapons than any other state worldwide and were the manufacturers of the largest nuclear bomb ever made.

'So, while they grow stronger the European forces grow weaker. They are planning to increase their influence in the eastern Mediterranean, expanding the naval base in Tartus in Syria to include a facility in Cyprus. They have expanded their naval facilities in the Black Sea with the annexation of the Crimea and they are beefing up their base in Kaliningrad in the Baltic by introducing new missiles that almost certainly contravene the INF treaty signed in 1987. They argue that their future expansion plan should be covered by the "maskirovka" principle in that areas where they have Russian speaking peoples, trained agitators will be sent in to destabilise the immediate area.

'Then gradually they will push further in to the area with Russians filling the void left by refugees, who will receive special grants to settle the vacated territory, much like the British did in the nineteenth century.' She looked up again. 'Nothing is new in this world.' she smiled.

'The immediate areas considered, are those where they have a pincer grip on the area,

Lithuania is a prime subject sitting between the Russian Baltic Sea State and Belarus who are friendly to Russia. The Leader of Lithuania is to be assassinated the blame being placed on the CIA and the reason given is the old one that still works perfectly well, that the US want to destabilise Lithuania so that Russia will be forced out of their South Baltic area.

'They plan for Belarus to squeeze the area to the west and they will then put heavy pressure on Latvia whose Russian citizens equal 25% of the total population. That would leave Estonia in the north high and dry. Done gradually, it's reasoned that the NATO countries wouldn't go to war over Lithuania, just as Europe didn't over Czechoslovakia in 1939. This incidentally is planned to be dealt with before the end of 2016, although the plan can be delayed depending upon circumstances.'

There was noticeable concern on people's faces around the table.

'The next step in their plans would be to see what could be achieved in Finland and Sweden neither of them being NATO countries. They are also gaining influence in old Soviet controlled countries such as Hungary where they have recently loaned US$10 billion for infrastructure purposes.

'The European Union has protested that Hungary has broken EU rules by introducing certain non-democratic methods into that country.

'At the same time Russia will be increasing their presence in the Black Sea area and the Aegean, Greece and the Greek Islands. The most interesting part of this report is the one

144

on China, Putin knows that China historically owned a good part of eastern Russia and if they are to expand their territorial interests, East Russia with its huge supply of valuable minerals would be an obvious strategic move.

'They also include in their report that in a recent secret meeting China has indicated interests in not only Taiwan, but Vietnam, Cambodia and India. The report finishes up by stating that by continuing to create a permanent enemy, it will keep control of the masses. Any dissidents will be quietly dealt with. Traitors will be hunted down wherever they may be and assassinated in a way that sends a message to others considering working against the regime. They state that there will be opportunities that are either created by their actions or by other means, which could be taken advantage of, in other words, waiting for an opportunistic situation.'

Mrs. Shaw took her glasses off. 'That's basically it in a nutshell; Putin is not going to stop, and the more powerful his military becomes, the more he will grasp. He recognises the weaknesses of the individual democratic states and like Hitler he will expose those weaknesses and use both diplomatic and military force and the threat to expand the Russian influence. We must also consider that Russia is not like Germany; a land that was arguably surrounded by potential enemies, Russia has a land depth that is unique in world.'

Bill Cummins thanked Mrs. Shaw. 'I guess this guy is playing Russian roulette with his people, it seems to me that we have to somehow get through to the ordinary Russian just what a dangerous gambler their President is.'

'The problem is,' said James Winston-Jones, that by keeping the Russian masses under strict control, the government can get away with an average wage equal to about US$550 per month. Add to this the huge amount of natural resources under their land mass, means that despite only having a GDP equal to that of South Korea he can afford to build and maintain a huge military structure. Because the social benefits are few in Russia, their debt is only about 12% against GDP, Britain is 85% and the USA 105%. Now he has the income from oil and gas reserves, he is able to maintain a low debt ratio.'

Bill Cummins nodded, 'it's true, but sanctions are starting to bite, and their reserves have been halved on the latest figures. I believe the biggest threat is the man himself, he's not getting any younger, but will want to leave a permanent legacy by increasing his power base.

'Now gentlemen, we have prepared the original report of some three thousand pages for our British friends and the original will be sent to Washington, but not to be widely distributed at this time, as the longer we can disguise the fact that we have these papers the better. We have already extracted the DNA from the Assassination copies, and it may well be that we can use these and perhaps the original report at a special meeting of the United Nations.

'In the meantime, I'll recommend that a précis should be sent to our NATO allies for them to think again before reducing their defence budgets.'

'What about the American Ambassador to Moscow?' George Manning asked.

Bill Cummins nodded, 'Well, that's above my pay grade, the documents will be sent to both the State Department and the CIA, but I'd imagine nothing will happen immediately, as to alert her may rather defeat the object of the exercise.'

The meeting carried on for a further two hours and ended up with both the British and the Americans consulting with their respective governments.

BELARUS

Chapter 16

George Manning spent the rest of his day writing up his own report, but he didn't finish it and decided to turn in early and finish it early the next day, when he expected to fly to Washington.

The next day, Sunday 24th May, George remembered that his case had been left in Donetsk as there was not room to carry it in the Apache. Apart from personal belongings, it contained all the cash he had drawn out.

The only item he had brought with him was his wallet with the debit card, and the passport for Timothy Shaw which was in his inside pocket, it not being possible to carry a bag with him on the Apache.

He spent the day relaxing and reading and on Monday 25th May, he called in to see Jim Wallace and told him that he didn't even have a change of clothes so he needed some cash to enable him to go down to Kiev and buy some clothes and other essentials.

Jim greeted him cordially and asked him to take a seat, coffee ordered, they discussed Saturday's meeting until the coffee came.

'Okay George, I'll get someone to go shopping for you, as it wouldn't be appropriate for you to be seen in Kiev, there are many prying eyes around here. Now, we have another problem.'

'Oh,' said George, surprised.

Jim Wallace looked grim, 'I'm very sorry George, but we can't send you back to the States.'

George felt anger rising in him as only the day before he'd received a promise that he would be able to get back to his wife who was still in Florida with the children.

'I need to get back to see my wife and children,' stated George, 'that's the least you guys can do for me, I've done more than my bit, and I feel that some R&R wouldn't go amiss.'

'Yes, you have George, much more than your bit as you call it, but a problem has surfaced this morning that could blow the whole thing apart.'

George raised his eyebrows.

'I've just received a message from Leond that he learned from a friend in the ex-General's office that Sherepov, wasn't killed in the explosion and he has carried out an investigation of all the bodies found on the site, and yours wasn't among them. He now suspects you may have got away, but now he believes you may still be in the Donetsk area.'

'Oh, shit,' said George.

'Yeah right, now this creates two problems, one is that they have intensified their searches in the area, which means that they may well uncover other things that we don't want them to and if nothing is found, they may assume that you escaped with the original documents, in which case our plans will be blown.'

George sighed, 'yes I can see the problem, but what's the solution?'

'My deputy Peter Lienster and I have had an idea, but I'm afraid it will involve you going back.'

'What, back to Donetsk?' said George incredulously.

'No George, let's get Peter in here and you can listen to his idea.'

Jim Wallace pressed a button on his intercom. 'Peter I've George with me now, looking rather unhappy I have to say,' he smiled at George, 'come up would you and tell him of your solution to our problem.'

Peter Lienster joined them in Jim Wallace's office a few minutes later.

He shook George's hand before sitting down.

'Okay, Jim will have told you of our problem.'

George nodded.

'We need to convince Sherepov that we don't have the documents, right?'

George frowned, 'I'm a little confused. As you now have the documents and clearly you can get them safely out of the country without any problem, why does it matter whether Russia knows we are in possession of them?'

'Ah yes, good question,' answered Peter, looking at Jim. 'If the Russians feel that they are successful in getting the documents back, they'll assume the problem will disappear and they can continue with their plans regarding the Baltic States and other areas. The assassination documents will prove to be a major embarrassment, but that is not the major factor here. Everyone knows that there's state murder in Russia, so that's no surprise. The fact that the documents include a secret report indicating China as the enemy in the long term would be a huge embarrassment to them and it would certainly sour current relations with that country.' Peter looked up from his notes. 'It would be akin to the Zimmerman telegram sent by Germany in the First World War, when they suggested to Mexico that Germany would help finance Mexico to attack Arizona and Texas. Russia's reference to a secret meeting with China where the latter expressed interest in not just Taiwan, Vietnam, Cambodia and India is dynamite. If we're to make the most out of this extraordinary piece of good luck it needs to be brought out into the open at a specific moment, either at the United Nations or,' Peter looked up again at Jim, 'to use it for some future negotiation soon.'

George nodded, 'you mean as blackmail for something we want?'

'Or something that we don't want Russia to do,' answered Jim. 'It's always useful to have a trump card up one's sleeve.'

'Okay Peter, I get the drift, please carry on.'

'For you to go back to the Donetsk area would be foolhardy and wouldn't achieve anything anyway. However, if you'd escaped through Belarus and made your way through to Vilnius the capital of Lithuania, that could be believable. You could claim that you were spirited across the war zone border by paying some smugglers; they would assume that you'd plenty of cash on you. You got to Kiev but instead of checking in at the embassy, you bought a car here and went via Belarus through Minsk to Vilnius. We can supply you with a Lithuanian passport and I know you speak passable Russian, so you could easily bluff your way through. When you arrive in Vilnius, you would book into an obscure hotel and contact the local political man at the Russian Embassy and tell him to contact Sherepov saying you have something of value that you want to exchange for cash.'

'The Package? But how...?'

'Okay, we've got a method here where we have made exact copies of the material. We have the DNA samples, and a courier has taken one of the 'X' documents to a Swiss Pharmaceutical company that is beyond repute so we can now allow the originals to be returned. They will arrive back by courier this evening. We can open an account for you at a major British Bank in Vilnius and you would go there and ask for a safe deposit box, where you would place the package.

'When you contact the Russian Embassy in Vilnius you should leave a message for Sherepov that you have the package and you'll hand it over for $1 million US, don't go in too heavy as they may consider other ways of getting it out.

'It's my view that he'll believe you're prepared to sell the documents, they always believe the worst of people. When you're contacted with their agreement, you say that you want the money transferred to an account in the Cayman Islands, we'll open a Barclays account for your there, and once the money is in your account, you'll send them the key to the deposit box. However, by that time you'll be on your way back to the States. Whatever you do, you mustn't agree to meet anyone.'

George thought for a minute. 'How difficult will it be getting through Belarus?'

'It should be no problem,' answered Jim Wallace, who'd just joined the meeting, 'although Lithuania is a member of NATO, they have trading agreements with Belarus, so the fact that a Lithuanian is travelling through the country will not be surprising to them. We'll invent some commodity that you'll be selling, and give you samples which you can give away. Perhaps toy drones or something they would find difficult to get over there. The whole area is completely corrupt so you could easily buy your way out of trouble if you ran into a problem.'

'How would I travel to the States on a Lithuanian passport?'

'We'd organise our embassy there to leave flexible tickets and an American passport in your name for you to pick up at the airlines desk.'

'Well you seem to have thought of everything, when would you want me to go?'

'Okay, I suggest you set off tomorrow morning before dawn. Just in case there are watchers outside the embassy we'll move you after dark tonight to the safe apartment house at 31 Turiviska. It will take you about 7 hours to reach Minsk and about a further 2 hours or so to get to Vilnius, you could do it one day, but I'd suggest you stay in Minsk for the night and drive to Lithuania the next morning, so it looks as though you had business in the area before moving on.'

'Is there any chance Belarus would have had my details circulated by the FSB?' asked George.

'Doubtful,' answered Peter, 'but I'll get our embassy there to check.'

'Okay,' said George resignedly, 'if someone can get me some change of clothes today that would help, by the way, what about a car?'

'Don't worry we've acquired a good second hand one here for cash under your name and you can just leave it in Lithuania when you've finished with it, if you leave it at the airport with the key on top of the rear drivers side wheel, we'll get it picked up by one of the embassy staff there.'

'Oh, one other thing,' said George, 'could you ask for the person who is making the purchases to get me a pay as you go mobile phone, mine is still in my case which is in the underground area near the farm.'

'I'll see to that George,' said Peter, 'can you think of anything else? A pretty woman perhaps,' he joked.

George laughed, 'just being with my wife would be nice,' he answered.

It was later in the day when Jim Wallace called George on the intercom positioned in the temporary office.

'George, can you come up to my office, I've a favour to ask.'

'Oh, oh,' thought George. He quickly finished off his report and walked up to the next floor to Jim Wallace's office.

As he walked in, he noticed Jim holding up a passport. 'This is for you George; it's the Lithuanian passport we promised you. Your name is Rolandas Giedrimas and you have a

154

wife and two children, your wife Carla is currently working in the United Kingdom. You won't need any other details, as you can say you are currently living in Ukraine working for Toyplus Exports Inc an American company that makes toys, and their newest line is radio-controlled drones. We'll make sure that you have some brochures to put in the car. There are also some business cards in there and your address in Kiev is an apartment at 31 Turiviska. It's a safe house owned by us, so no problems there and the business number would be transferred to us here in case anyone checks.'

George took the passport. 'You said you wanted a favour....'

'Ah, yes George. Bill Cummins had totally forgotten that Diedre Robinson, one of our senior diplomatic assistants, has been transferred to Lithuania, she was due to leave next Saturday but it struck us that she could accompany you it would give you some extra cover. You did say you'd like a pretty woman with you,' he smiled, 'a man and woman travelling together might be more acceptable and as she has a diplomatic passport, it may help in case of problems.'

'I think it was Peter who suggested a pretty woman,' George said, 'yes of course I would be happy to have the company, but are you expecting problems?' asked George.

Jim Wallace laughed, 'expect the worst and hope for the best, is my motto George. The answer to your question is no, but it's important you make it through. Diedre will be briefed about what you're doing, so you'll be able to rely on her to give you support should you need it.'

George nodded. 'Okay, when do I meet Deirdre?'

'I'll call her now.' Jim picked up the intercom phone, 'Ah Miss Robinson, Mr. Manning has agreed for you to accompany him, so perhaps you would like to meet him?'

She said she would be right up and George sat back in his chair.

'What about driving licences and insurance certificates for the car?'

'All those documents including all the bank details you'll need will be in the glove box, including ownership receipts, but you should check them as soon as the car is delivered,' answered Jim Wallace.

'And the type of car?'

'It's a Mercedes G-Class 4x4, so if you need to turn off the highway, you'll have no problem.'

There was a knock on the door and Diedre walked in. George had expected a wispy young woman with rimless glasses, why he didn't quite know. Diedre was not like his original vision at all. He gasped at the apparition in front of him. She was very good looking with full slightly downward pointing lips, dark, almost black hair, which, cut short accentuated the blue eyes that shone with intelligence from a perfect complexion. She was dressed smartly in a dark blue suit with a white blouse. She walked confidently up to George and shook his hand. 'It's good to meet you Mr. Manning,' she smiled.

George laughed out loud which puzzled Jim Wallace. 'The name is George, and it's good to meet you, ty govoris' po-russki? (Do you speak Russian?)'

'Da,' (Yes).

That's good, do you drive?'

'Da,'

George smiled, 'that's good too we can share the driving. Perhaps it would be a good idea if you packed this evening and placed your bags in the car, and so that we get to know each other a little better we could have an early dinner,' he smiled.

'Yes, that's great,' Diedre answered, 'here's my telephone number, just let me know where to meet you and I'll get a cab.'

'Ah, I've just had a thought,' said George. 'Perhaps as it's important that I shouldn't be seen, do you think you could bring around a couple of takeaways to my apartment at 31 Turiviska? Jim here has said that I am to be spirited there as soon as it's dark.'

Diedre laughed, 'you sure know how to treat a girl on a night out,' she joked, 'yes will do. I'll come around at eight.'

She went to leave the office and as she reached the door, she turned, 'Oh, by the way I'll be carrying an automatic in my handbag, but if you're also carrying one, we should find a better place to put them.'

George nodded, 'I'll think of a place when I've seen the car, see you later Diedre.'

The door shut.

'Okay George, good luck.' Jim Wallace stood up behind his desk and held out his hand.

George took it and thanked him, saying that he would contact him when they reached Lithuania.

He left the office and went back to the one he was using to clear his desk.

When he left Jim Wallace's office, Jim picked up the internal phone.

'Bill?'

Bill Cummins answered. 'Hi Jim, I assume you've briefed George? Yeah, now tell me, Diedre wasn't scheduled for Lithuania, was she?'

There was a silence on the line for a moment. 'No.'

'So, what gives Jim?'

Jim laughed, 'She's one of our "Treasury people" from Washington,' he lied, 'and they want to make sure that George does what we've told him to do. She works for a completely different department, very secret, so she's not known to me or anyone else here in fact she only flew in this morning.'

Bill frowned, 'Well, even if he were crooked, he wouldn't be so stupid to defect with his wife and children still in Florida.'

'Well what he has in his hands is worth a lot of cash, but I agree with you, we've no reason to believe that he is in any way dishonest, but Mary Clancy was killed so there's just the outside possibility that George was implicated in her murder.'

'I don't see it Jim,' answered Bill Cummins, 'he wouldn't have brought us the information he did if he was working for the other side.'

'Unless the information was altered to throw us off the scent...'

'But what about the assassination documents with signatures and we now know that the DNA we retrieved from those documents belonged to the person who signed them.'

'We don't,' answered Jim Wallace.

'Hang about Jim I was assured by you that we had the correct DNA.'

Jim nodded, 'yeah that's what I was told, but since then we realised the person who brought back a glass from a diplomatic banquet that was used by the target, was the American Ambassador to Moscow, Emilie Dixon.'

'Jesus, so if we can't be sure, how can we verify the documents?'

'We can't without someone getting another smear, but that's not going to be easy in the short term.'

'But George now has the original documents...'

'Yeah, we had no choice but to return them, but we have the DNA from those anyway so if we get a match, we'll know we're okay.'

Bill Cummins sat back in his chair in thought. 'Okay, so if this is a devious Russian trick, how are we going to assess the situation?'

'It's difficult, if Russia pays to get the documents back, then we still don't know, and they'd do that anyway to keep up the pretence.'

'So, either way, whether they pay or not doesn't tell us anything.'

'That's right, and we don't know at this stage whether the American Ambassador to Washington is working for us or the other side either.'

'Or it's George Manning that's the traitor, or both?'

'That's right Bill, the only way we're going to know is if George "lights up" Belarus security, that's one thing or alternatively if he gets through without any problems, he's got to be suspect, because we know Sherepov sent to the security apparatus in Belarus details of him.'

'But if Sherepov did that, surely that indicates that George is in the clear as far as we are concerned.'

'Not necessarily Bill that could be part of the plot.'

'Okay Jim, what if anything is going to demonstrate that George is in the clear?'

'One, if we find that the DNA, we currently hold is false, which then almost certainly implicates the current American Ambassador to Moscow.'

'But even then, it doesn't clear George Manning.'

'No, but if George has problems in Belarus that will give an indication he may be in the clear, as it's improbable that they would go after him otherwise.'

'You mean if he's killed by them?'

'Hmm, doubtful that they would kill him either way, but that's why Deirdre is with him,'

'What exactly is her role in all this Jim?'

'One, to make an assessment as to whether George is clean, two to assist him if they have problems, as I've intimated, she is not quite what she appears to be and three to ensure the money goes to the right account in Cayman. If George passes all those tests, then we must assume he is truly one of us, but as you know Bill when dealing in any sort of espionage, it's the "balance sheet" over a period that gives one confidence.'

Bill Cummins nodded, 'yes I understand that, but looking at George's record of military service, and his job in Ukraine and subsequently in Moscow, my bet is that he's a patriot.'

'Yes, I agree on the balance of probabilities, but we have to be sure,' said Jim.

Bill Cummins put the phone down. He guessed which department Diedre worked for. 'Thank God I'm not in intelligence,' he said to his secretary who'd been listening in.

As soon as Jim had finished talking to Bill Cummins, he buzzed his secretary. 'Joan, I believe there's a Mr. Shininsky waiting to see me, show him up would you.'

A few minutes later, a large man with a rumpled suit entered his office and was ushered to a seat, 'Boris, both you and Mikhail have been briefed?'

'Yes sir,' he answered with a heavy Eastern European accent.

'Good, your job is to follow George Manning; he has had a tracking device attached to his car, so you can allow him to be out of sight. Any problems you are to intervene, there is no way you can allow him to be captured, is that clear?'

'And if he has no problems?'

'Leave that to Diedre, I'm sure she has her instructions.'

On Tuesday 26th May George Manning and Diedre Robinson set out at just after 04:00 hours, they crossed the Ukrainian/Belarus border about three hours later just south of Stolin. There were no problems and they headed north-west for Pinsk with the idea of getting on to the E30 for Minsk. They'd just passed Ivatsevichi when Diedre's mobile rang. George who was still driving looked at her with raised eyebrows.

'Yes, copy that,' she said to the caller, 'we'll divert ASAP and contact you later.' Diedre looked at her watch, it was 10:30.

She turned to George, 'okay, Jim has just been informed that GCHQ in the UK, who are monitoring our course, have picked up a message that the Stolin border police have reported that we passed through there about an hour ago heading towards Pinsk. As a result, there are now two police vehicles headed out of Minsk travelling south at speed on this road.'

'In that case there's no way we can stay overnight in Minsk as planned,' said George.

'Right, I want you to take the next left towards Slonim and before we reach Slonim, we'll hang a left onto the P99 towards Selva. Just before Selva we'll turn right towards Dziarecyn and then left on the P41 towards Masty. Once we get on that road it's heavily forested and we can get off road if necessary, the forest would cover us if they use choppers.'

'You appear to have alternatives well sorted out,' said George, 'particularly efficient for an assistant secretary.' He glanced at her and smiled; 'of course you're not just an assistant secretary, are you?' he goaded her. Diedre just smiled. They reached the left turn and George swung off the E30 headed for Slonim.

'What about road blocks?'

Diedre nodded, 'it's likely they'll organise those later, now they'll hope to catch us on the

E30, so we have about an hour before there's a full alert.' She looked at her watch. 'We should be close to Masty by then, and from there it's about another hour to the border with Lithuania.'

'But there's bound to be a welcoming committee at all the border posts,' said George.

'Which is why we're going to head for the Aziory area, there's thick foliage between there and the border, so we'll take the cross-country route which will avoid the border posts. Don't worry George, we'll get to where we're supposed to be, this is not the first time I've travelled this route. You should also be aware that we have two sweepers behind us, just in case we run into difficulties.'

George knew that Diedre was accompanying him not just to give him support, but also to check on his veracity, but he was comfortable with his passenger. He wondered what sort of end game they expected from her if she'd decided against him. He put those thoughts out of his mind as he drove faster towards Slonim. When they reached a part of the road that had a small diversion, presumably designed for tired drivers to pull in, Diedre asked him to stop, he did so, and she jumped out of the car opening the boot and taking out a pair of licence plates giving one to George along with a screwdriver. 'Just a precaution George, you change the front plates and I'll deal with the rear.' It took only a few minutes to make the change and Diedre took the old plates and threw them over a hedge.

'Do you want me to drive George?' she asked.

George shook his head, 'negative Diedre, you look after the route.'

'Okay,' she said, 'the paperwork for the new plates are in my hand bag, so if we're stopped, don't give them the stuff you have in the glove box. On the left-hand side of you is a lever, if you pull it up, it will raise a piece of heavy gauge metal in the back that'll give some protection if we have to run through a road block.'

George looked surprised, 'I thought this was a second-hand vehicle?'

'Yes, but suitably modified, it was only completed late yesterday afternoon.' she smiled.

They reached the P99 road and George took the turn towards Selva.

Diedre's mobile rang again. 'Yes, okay I have that, what should we expect?'

She switched off. 'Things are hotting up George, they have now realised that we've not taken the Minsk road, and they have put out a general alert, which means road blocks.' Diedre unfolded the map on her lap. 'Okay, I would expect a block just before the junction when I'd planned to turn right onto the P142 which would take us to the P41 and Masty. In about 15 kilometres we'll come to a track on the right, we'll take that and cut off the corner. This vehicle; designed for rough ground, should be no problem. It's also a wooded area, which will give us some cover in case there's an air search. Then we'll take a left off the P142 before we get to Dziarecyn and cut off another corner. They won't be expecting us to use rough ground, so we should be able to make progress and reach just short of Masty. Then we have a problem.'

'What's that?' asked George.

'There's the River Nemunas that runs through Masty and cuts across our path, so we have no choice but to go over one of the bridges, and they are bound to have road blocks.'

'Do you have a solution?'

'Yeah, we'll stop off in a wooded area just before the P41 joins with the P51 and I'll get our followers to run through the area and see what we're facing. They'll be able to reconnoitre the two bridges and report back. I was hoping we'd be able to get through Masty before the balloon went up.'

'Okay, you just tell me where to stop, and we'll pull out the thermos of coffee and sandwiches.' smiled George.

The plan worked, they pulled off the road skirting Zelva. Diedre suggested she drive as any vehicle coming the other way would be looking for a male driver and a different registration number. They switched over just before joining the P142 and Diedre sped north towards Dziarecyn. As planned, she pulled off the road to the left and skirted the town.

Joining the P41, they then headed towards Masty and about 30 minutes later they pulled off the main road into a culvert that was well hidden from the road, Diedre contacted the car behind on her encrypted phone.

'Boris, you know where we are?'

'Yes.'

'Good, I need you to do some forward reconnaissance, go past us and let us know what's ahead.'

'Understood, out.'

An hour later they were conscious of a vehicle stopping nearby and shortly Boris scrambled down the bank into the culvert. He opened the rear door and climbed in.

'Okay, there's a road block at Masty but the road is clear on the intersections leading to the P51 north towards Shchuchhyn. My suggestion is that you turn left before reaching Shchuchhyn, which will take you to the M6, go straight across into the wooded area to meet the P51 again further north towards Astryna. From there you can head north on the road to Radun, go through Radun onto the P135 then left at Paharodna and left again onto H1604. This road has been destroyed at the border, so there is no border post there. You may be able to get through with this vehicle, if not try to cross over by foot and we'll meet you at the other side, but it'll take us a while to get around to meet you. There's a possibility that the area is mined and /or there is a secure fence in which case we'll have to re think how we'll get you across.

'There are several decent B roads from there, but you've got your map, so it should be no problem. Just one warning though, there are regular patrols particularly on the Lithuanian side as the border is particularly sensitive now and they will have no hesitation in shooting to kill.'

Deirdre asked one or two questions and seemed satisfied with the answers.

'I suggest we change roles,' suggested Boris, 'we'll let you have our tracking device and we'll take the tracker off your vehicle. This way we will lead a mile or so ahead and if we meet any problems, we can let you know so you'll have time to get out of the way, in the event of a road block. We'll go through the road block and return via a different direction.'

Boris was just climbing back up the culvert when he heard the screaming of a police siren. He'd just reached the road, when the police vehicle stopped by their car.

There were two officers, both got out and walked towards them.

'What were you doing out of your car?' one asked, the other was walking around their vehicle, peering inside.

'I was having a pee.' laughed Boris, 'What do you think I was doing?'

The policeman was not amused. 'Where have you come from?' He was eyeing the Ukrainian number plates on the car.

'We're Ukrainian, travelling to Vilnius in Lithuania,' answered Boris.

'Your papers please,' asked the second policeman. Boris and Mikhail produced their passports which were carefully looked at and then given back.

'Why are you going to Lithuania?' asked the first policeman.'

Boris shrugged, 'we have business there, legal business.' he added.

The second policeman then produced a picture of George Manning. 'Have you seen this man?'

Boris looked at the picture carefully and shook his head, passing it to Mikhail. 'He doesn't look Ukrainian to me,' said Mikhail, 'that's a very expensive suit he's wearing.'

The first policemen nodded, 'he's travelling under a Lithuanian passport, but he's an American spy who's wanted for murder.'

'Murder.' repeated Boris frowning, 'What's he doing in this part of the world?'

The police were tiring of the questioning clearly, they thought they were wasting their time with these two fellows, and were eager to get on their way.

'Okay, if you see him, he's with an attractive woman, you must contact us immediately,' Boris was handed a telephone number to call. With that they climbed into their car and left headed north-west, the same direction Boris and Mikhail were heading.

Boris watched them go until they were out of sight and then vaulted over the hedge into the culvert and tapped at the side window. Diedre opened it.

'Yes, we heard the police siren,' she smiled, 'but I assume you have sent them on their way?'

Boris nodded, 'Yeah, they have gone but unfortunately in same direction we're all headed, and by the way George, they say you're wanted for murder.'

George rolled his eyes upwards, 'hmm, well in for a penny in for a pound as my English colleagues would say, but I guess it's obvious they'll paint as black a picture as they can.'

'Yeah, I guess so, well we'll have to stick to our original plan, so here's the tracking device, I've just taken the tracker from underneath your vehicle, so I suggest you sit about two miles behind, as those guys may return, and you'll need warning if they do. I know you have a secure phone Diedre, but we don't and whilst it's unlikely that they are sophisticated enough to pick up our calls, you never can tell, so whatever we say on the phone will be brief and to the point.'

'Okay, got it,' answered Diedre.

Boris disappeared back over the hedge, and they heard their vehicle start and drive away.

'I'll give them about ten minutes,' said Diedre, 'then we'll follow.'

Ten minutes later, she negotiated her way out of the culvert and back onto the main road. 'If the police car comes back down the road, we may not have time to move away as the area where we have to travel is not wooded and there's little other cover,' she said.

George agreed and said that he would duck below the dashboard so that they would only see her driving. 'With the new registration plates, they would probably ignore us.'

It was only another fifteen minutes that had gone by, when Diedre's phone rang. George answered it.

'Yes.'

'It's Boris, our enemy has turned around and is heading your way at high speed we'll follow at a distance to give help if needed.'

'Roger.'

'Did you hear that Diedre?'

'Yeah, check the sky; are there any aircraft up there?'

George looked around. 'Jesus, there's a chopper about a mile away, they must have spotted us. Doubtful that they are certain it's

169

us who they are after, but the car's the same, even if the registration isn't, so they'll have reported that fact.'

'Is it a military aircraft?' asked Diedre.

George looked again, 'no it's a Jet Ranger, probably a police unit.'

'Okay, so they'll only have small arms on board,' said Diedre.

'I wish we'd had one of those Stingers the Brits had as part of their equipment, I'd feel more comfortable that we could defend ourselves...'

'Don't worry George, Boris and Mikhail are well armed, and they have something similar hidden in their vehicle if they have to use it.'

The road at this stage was very straight, so they had plenty of time to see the police car hurtling towards them. About a quarter of a mile from them the car swerved across the road and the policemen got out both sporting sub-machine guns. They spaced themselves out, one at the rear of their car and the other in front, both looking extremely menacing.

Diedre slowed down and drove to about 100 yards of the police car where she stopped. She realised that she could just about get past either side of them, but not without suffering hits from at least one of the sub-machine guns firing at them. George also noticed the Jet Ranger helicopter was approaching at speed and dropping in height as it did so.

She told George to stay put as she got out of the car and went around to the boot, opening it and extracting what looked like a small package, which she'd had in an overnight case.

As she was walking towards the police car, she used her mobile to phone Boris and told him of their position.

Boris confirmed that he was dealing with the situation and would be with them within about five minutes.

As she got closer to the police, they both armed their guns. Diedre put her hands in the air, still holding the package in her right hand.

'What have got in the package?' asked one of them.

'$5,000 US,' she said sweetly as she closed with them. 'Look, I realise you're doing your duty, but the man in the car is no murderer, he is American and he's a diplomat, but the matter is political. If you take the $5,000, I am holding and let us go, no one will know, you know how valuable US dollars are in Belarus...' Just then there was a huge explosion in the sky as the police helicopter exploded and dropped to the ground about a kilometre to Diedre's right.

Both men felt the force of the explosion, even where they were standing.

They were severely shaken, but nevertheless kept their guns trained on Diedre. They realised however that with the demise of the helicopter no one would know if they accepted the bribe. The more senior of the men spoke. 'I think we can simply take your $5,000 and still apprehend the fugitive, what is to stop us?' he grinned evilly, thinking that his day had come at last.

'There's just one thing to stop you doing that,' said Diedre.'

'Oh, and what's that?' asked the second man.

'If you look closely,' said Diedre, 'you'll see that I am holding something with the package of money, it's a hand grenade, and the pin has been removed. Any attempt by either of you to take the money would certainly kill us all and the money would also be blown to smithereens. Now do we have a deal or not?' A note of urgency came into her voice.

Just then a car drew up from the opposite direction, and the second policeman waved it through. As it drew level it stopped. The policemen were irritated and told the driver to move. Boris wound his window down and poked out an Uzi machine gun. Mikhail had opened the door at the other side and climbed out training his Uzi on the two men.

'I would suggest you put your weapons down.' said Diedre softly, 'we're not here to kill anyone. The deal I gave you is still on offer, but make up your minds quickly please.'

The two policemen realised they'd little choice if they wanted to escape with their lives; the bringing down of the police helicopter was an indication that the people they were facing were not amateurs.

They both put their weapons down on the tarmac, and Mikhail sprinted forward and picked them up.

'We should kill them,' said Mikhail.

'No,' answered Diedre in English, 'there is no need, once they accept the money they will be compromised, and we still have to get out of this wretched country. The helicopter crash could have been due to an engine failure and it'll take them some time to assess what really happened, but if we take out these two, it will be quickly determined that there is someone

172

wandering around their country with serious intent. The last thing we want at this stage is for them to call in their military as that would be a game changer.'

While Diedre was discussing the matter with Boris, the two policemen were talking to each other in whispers.

'We accept your offer,' said the senior policemen after conferring with his junior partner.

Diedre handed the package of cash over to him. 'Now, Mikhail you can unload their weapons and let them take them back, otherwise they would have difficulty in answering questions as to where they lost them. The same thing with the magazines, wrap those in a bag with Sellotape and stick those in the boot of their car.' She turned to the two policemen. 'The cash is real but the numbers have been recorded, should you consider reporting that you've seen us without of course mentioning the money you've received, we will let the authorities know that you were bribed and prove that by releasing the numbers on the notes.'

The senior policeman nodded, 'No, you can be sure that we haven't seen you, end of story.'

At that moment George got out of the car and walked up to where Diedre was standing. 'I gather you've everything under control,' he smiled, 'what's the plan?'

Diedre replaced the pin in the hand grenade, and handed it to George, 'there are a bunch of them in my overnight bag, I suggest you put this one back, but move the bag onto the back seat, I've a feeling we may need them.'

The policemen took their empty weapons back, got into their car and sped off towards Zelva.

'Okay,' said Diedre, now taking complete control of the operation. 'We need to get out of here fast, as the ungodly will be coming to find out what's happened to their chopper. Let's go back to our original plan, you lead Boris, we'll follow behind as before. We're only about 70 kilometres from the border, so let's go.'

She waited about two minutes to let Boris get ahead and then started the motor. George noticed that Boris was driving rather faster and mentioned this fact to Diedre. She put her foot further down and at about 140 kpm, George reported that they were now keeping pace. They took the diversion that skirted Shchuchhyn and crossed the M6 joining the P51 again towards Astryna. Boris reported that there were no roadblocks around the small town, and they headed north on the P142 as planned, they were now headed towards Radun. About half way there, Diedre's phone rang and George picked it up.

'We've just been passed by two off road police vehicles heading towards you at high speed, how far are you from your turn off?'

George grabbed the map from the back of the car and opened it.

'I guess we're about 10 kilometres away from where we were going to turn off, but we can turn off at Zabalac which is about 5 kilometres north of us.'

'Okay, I think they may see you because it's such a straight road, you'll just have to make a run for it, it's pretty wooded up there so you should have plenty of cover. We're turning around now and we'll follow up behind to make sure you get through but that area is heavily fenced on the border, so you won't get through with the vehicle, we'll aim to pick you up at the other side.'

Boris was correct, although they reached the left turn shortly afterwards, they could see the police vehicles about half a kilometre up the road, and it was obvious that they'd be seen.

SHEREPOV INTERVENES

Chapter 17

The major picked up the phone and gave instructions regarding the continuance of the search.

'So Major, if George Manning had not been blown up in the large explosion, where is he likely to be?' asked Sherepov.

'He could have escaped across the firing line between the dissidents and the Ukrainian forces,' said the Major.

'Hmm, unlikely, it would be too risky, I'm getting reports that both sides are so trigger happy that they have been shooting each other. No, George Manning is not a fool, I've been in touch with our people in Kiev and they tell me that Manning hasn't been seen turning up at the American Embassy there. I've had a careful watch kept on the airport in Kiev and we've checked all the hotels. So, for the moment, let us assume that he didn't reach Kiev, what other route would he take?'

'Well,' said the Major, 'from what you've told me the files he has stolen are obviously very valuable...'

Sherepov slapped his hand on his knee and winced as he did so, it being his wounded leg. 'Of course, I should have foreseen the possibility from the start.'

The Major looked mystified.

'You're right Major the documents he holds are very valuable indeed, but only to us and the Americans. We're the only ones who would pay cash to get them back. Manning would have realised that, in which case, Kiev would have been the last place he would head for.'

'Where else would he head for?' asked the Major frowning.

'He wouldn't have headed south he would aim for the west either Poland or Lithuania via Belarus. Now if he'd gone north from here, he would have skirted the fighting zone. To get into Poland is a possibility, but he would know that we've many assets in Lithuania. I wonder, would he have taken the chance to get there via Belarus which is a shorter route.' he continued, 'I'll get my people in Moscow to contact Poland, Belarus, and Lithuania to put out that we have a murderer on the run and for them to send details of George Manning. There's little point in giving his name, he'll almost certainly be travelling under a false passport,' he said almost to himself, 'but a photograph and the reward should be circulated.

'I've the feeling Major, that if we don't catch him here, we may well hear from him before long. However, in the meantime continue your search it may be that he's just keeping low.'

The Major got up and saluted. 'I'll keep you informed of anything we pick up in this area sir.'

THE SURPRISE

Chapter 18

Diedre swung off the main road at Sabalac and kept her eye on the rear-view mirror, to her surprise it appeared that the police vehicles hadn't followed them. Boris suggested they stop at an appropriate place so that they could catch them up and discuss what they'd do next, George quickly confirmed this.

Diedre came across a small side road and turned into it to await Boris and Mikhail who joined them after five minutes.

Boris and Mikhail got out of their car, Mikhail climbed on top of a hedge, which gave him a view of the road behind while Boris climbed into the back of the Mercedes.

'They,' he jerked his thumb in the direction of Zabalac, 'must have been heading to where the chopper came down,' he said.

Diedre nodded, 'I guess so, because they must have seen us before we turned at Zabalac.'

'The question is, what we should do from here,' said George. 'The border isn't far, but I would imagine the border fence will be pretty difficult to circumvent and we don't know whether the area is mined.'

'We could blow the fence with the grenades,' said Diedre, 'but you're right, we have no way of detecting mines.'

Boris leaned forward from the rear. 'The fence is double skinned and grenades may not be enough. I reckon the only safe way to get you across is by chopper, what I suggest is that you drive into the forest, camouflage the car with bushes and then call us on your secure phone with your coordinates. You'll need to get as close as possible to the border to avoid any interception by the Belarus forces. We'll go through the main route and cross via the border post, once through we'll organise a Jet Ranger through the embassy and come and get you.'

'Yeah, I reckon that's by far the safest plan, Boris, how long do you reckon that'll take?' asked Diedre.

'Allow for 24 hours max, but we'll try to do much better than that, we have to cross over and then get to Vilnius, arrange the chopper and then fly to get you.'

'Are you licensed to fly?' asked Diedre.

'Yeah, I was a pilot for the Ukraine air force so no problem in trying to find someone who'd cross the border.'

'Alright,' said George, 'let's work to that plan, if we find we can get through without your help, we'll let you know.'

Boris got out of the car, 'I've got a Stinger missile unit and one missile left hidden under our car, which I'll transfer to you, I doubt you'll need it, but it wouldn't be helpful to have that gear on board, if they decide to search the car at the border post.'

'Yeah okay, stick it in the boot,' said George, 'we'll give you ten minutes to get well clear before we move.'

'You'll have to drop the back seat,' said Diedre, 'the Stinger is around five feet long.'

Mikhail sounded the all clear from the top of the hedge, he came down and helped Boris transfer their handguns and the Stinger to the Mercedes, and they drove off heading back towards Zabalac.

'Well, I guess we're on our own now,' George smiled at Diedre. He opened the map in front of him. 'The quicker we get to a hide, the better, I suggest we move along this road for about 2 kilometres. The road then goes through a thick wooded area, if we can find a good place to put the vehicle on the left-hand side, the border at the northern edge of the wood is within one and a half kilometres, easily walk-able. Of course, it may mean shacking up in the Mercedes overnight.'

Diedre nodded, 'I've been in worse places,' she laughed as she started the car.

It took only a few minutes to reach the wood and George said he would get out and walk in front of the car to enable him to reconnoitre. He soon came to a clearing and he waved Diedre in to it, she then drove the Mercedes into the thick brush on the far side. When she'd stopped, she had difficulty in getting the door open, but when she did so, walking back into the clearing, she realised that the Mercedes was completely covered.

'That's great Diedre,' complimented George, 'there's no way anyone is going to find that in a hurry. Now, if you're agreeable, I suggest we walk up to the edge of the forest, in sight of the border and we can take some coordinates with your phone.'

Diedre nodded, 'First I'm going to grab a sandwich which I brought for us and a drink of water then we'll head off. I'm afraid the car is looking a bit dirty after all the off-road running,' Diedre smiled.'

George looked at her surprised.

Diedre laughed, 'You see it's an offence in Belarus to have dirty vehicle...'

'You're joking,' said George.

'No, it's a fact.'

'Well we'll put that right before we go,' George laughed, 'we wouldn't want to break the law, would we?'

As they were walking through the forest, George turned to Diedre. 'I assume you had orders to eliminate me if it appeared that I was working for the other side?'

Diedre smiled, 'I never deal with hypothetical questions George, but you know the drill. It was difficult for Jim Wallace to know whether it was you or the American Ambassador to Moscow who was complicit in Mary's murder, certainly if you'd had an easy ride through Belarus it would have been a point against you, but there are other reasons for Jim's plan as you'll find out in due course. Of course, I knew you were kosher, but I couldn't break my cover to Jim Wallace. You know the department I'm responsible to are totally separate from the one you work for.'

'The blind leading the blind,' smiled George.

'Well, it's sometimes necessary that one part of the CIA doesn't know what the other is up to...'

Just as Diedre was speaking, George noticed some tracks in the wood, and he held his hand up.

'Hang on a minute Diedre, look at these tracks.'

Diedre looked, 'I wonder...'

'Jesus, these are tank tracks,' said George, 'and there is a hell of a lot of them.'

Altering their pace, they turned left following the tracks and suddenly they came upon an extraordinary sight. Within the cover of the wood, just short of the border were a line of tanks to the right and the left of where they stood.

'Let's follow these to the northern edge,' said George. When they reached the edge of the forest, they'd passed over fifty tanks.

George frowned, 'do you realise Diedre that if there are the same number the other side from where we walked there are at least one hundred tanks under cover.'

Diedre nodded, 'and no one around, that seems strange.'

'Hmm, well they have been hidden here for a purpose,' said George. He turned and looked at the insignia on the rear of the last tank. 'they are Russian, by God.' he exclaimed, 'now what the hell are Russian tanks doing near the Belarus/ Lithuanian border?'

'Well, they have not been here for too long,' said Diedre, 'the tracks are relatively fresh.'

'Yeah, but there are none outside the wood, so they are carefully positioned to ensure they are not seen from the air, which is probably why the fields have been ploughed.'

Diedre agreed.

'But this is a relatively small forest,' said George, 'do you realise that if they have used the other forest areas near the border in a similar way, they could have over two thousand tanks hidden.'

'Perhaps we should walk further and see...'

'No Diedre, we'd have to walk over open ground and that's too dangerous, they must have patrols out. No, our job is to get back and report our findings; this is a job for special services. But it does tend to put this whole thing into a new perspective.'

Boris and Mikhail drove back on to the main road turning left at Zabalac and headed north straight for Radun on the P145. Passing through Radun they veered right onto the P135 and then left on the E85 heading straight for Bieniakoni the last town before the Belarus / Lithuania border. As they approached the border crossing, there seemed to be few cars awaiting clearance with the normal line of trucks on the side road pending inspection. Boris moved their vehicle up the short queue until they were the next in line. He could clearly see the Lithuanian border guards waiting for the next car to go through.

What he saw next set his heart racing. He heard police sirens behind him and looking in his mirror saw the two vehicles he'd seen earlier bearing down on the border post. Boris's sixth sense told him that this was not good news. The border guard who was examining their passports had handed them back, and he turned to them with the instruction 'wait' seeing that the soldiers were distracted by the approaching vehicles, he quickly drove round the barrier and pressed down the accelerator. He saw the sudden look of alarm from the border guard in his rear mirror, but the man was far too late to react and by the time he thought about Boris and Mikhail they were approaching the Lithuanian border post where they stopped with a screech of tyres.

A Lithuanian border guard stuck his head through the car window. 'You guys in a hurry?' he asked.

'Yeah,' answered Boris, 'sorry about that.'

The guard nodded, 'well you're lucky to get through. We've just had a message that they have closed the border both ways.'

Boris breathed in heavily, 'okay, thanks are we clear to go?'

He checked their passports asked a couple of questions and said, 'Of course,' he stepped back from the vehicle and Boris gunned the engine again putting as much space as possible between the Belarus border post and themselves, only breathing easily when he turned the corner and was out of sight.

'Jesus, that was close,' said Mikhail. Boris nodded 'Yeah, it's hotting up over there, we need to get George and Diedre out ASAP.' He pulled over and stopped the car.

'Okay Mikhail, you drive, I need to make some phone calls.'

They got out of the car, and swapped seats, Mikhail starting the Mercedes heading for Vilnius.

Boris punched a number into his mobile and waited.

'Carrie Thompson, can I help you?'

'Yeah, Carrie this is Boris...'

'Yes, I know who you are by your number, but give me your date of birth please.'

'25101939,' It wasn't his date of birth of course but a pre-arranged code.

'Got it,' answered Carrie, 'Jim Wallace has been in touch, so no need to fill me in, are the "parcels" safe?' she was referring to George and Diedre.

'For the moment affirmative, but action is required.'

'Do you have a suggestion?' asked Carrie.

'Affirmative, I need a Jet Ranger to be hired from Vilnius airport, to pick up within two hours, fully fuelled.'

'With pilot?'

'Negative, I'm licensed.'

'Okay, I'll call you back.' The phone went dead.

'How long to get to Vilnius Airport,' Mikhail asked.

Boris looked at his watch, 'about 50 minutes, but we'll need to spend some time on the maps, and we'll have to await Diedre's call with the coordinates, she'll probably send those via SMS but she may send them direct to the embassy.'

After about thirty minutes Boris's phone rang, he pressed the receive button.

'Carrie?'

'Yes, small problem, no Jet Ranger available until this evening, I'll meet you at the airport in thirty minutes and you can fill me in with your intentions. I'll be at the Air Lituanica Desk or nearby.'

'OK, out.'

Boris drove into the airport area and they parked the car in the short-term car park. Mikhail stayed in the car with the phone and Boris walked into the airport proper, he soon spotted Carrie standing near the Lituanica desk. She was tall with short dark brown hair. A little too heavily made up for Boris's liking, but well-groomed and wore a smart green outfit. He reckoned her age at around thirty-five years old.

'Carrie?' asked Boris.

She smiled, 'the same,' she shook his hand.

'Let's go over there,' she pointed, 'to the coffee bar, so we can talk.'

They found a table in the corner and Carrie ordered two cappuccinos, delivered promptly.

'Okay, shoot.' Carrie took a sip of her coffee.

Boris explained everything that had happened since they crossed the border from Ukraine, Carrie already knew the reason for the trip.

'We left Diedre and George near the border, and the idea was for them to hide the vehicle they were using in the wooded area. Diedre, who has a secure phone, said she would call us with the coordinates of where they wanted a pick up.'

Carrie nodded, 'okay, I've got the coordinates which I received just before I left the embassy, but are you going in during daylight or when it's dark because Diedre gave me a warning code, which means that there are "bandits" nearby?'

'Ah, we thought the area was pretty well deserted,' answered Boris.

Carrie shook her head, 'it doesn't appear so.'

'Okay, then I suggest we do a night trip, they have a flash-light in the car, so they can send me a Morse signal that simply says OK, "dash-dash-dash, dash dot dash" if it's not OK tell 'em to send dash-dash-dash three times, then we'll stay well clear and try again in say 30 minutes. Because choppers are noisy buggers, we'll go down there early and park out of sight opposite the border, so that we'll only take about 3 or 4 minutes to pick 'em up and the time spent over the border will be even shorter. The fact that we start from nearby will mean that they won't be able to track us. There is just one request I'd make though.'

'Name it,' said Carrie.

'Well, if something goes wrong, we need a 4x4 vehicle standing by with a driver.'

'Do you want him armed with an RPG to blast a hole in the fence?' asked Carrie.

'No, it wouldn't help, firstly because I now know the fence is doubled along the border and secondly, we suspect it's mined, so we have to go in with the chopper, there's no other way. But if the "bandits", that is the Belarus army are nearby, they may take a shot at us.'

'Okay, I'll relay all this to Diedre. Time-line?'

'I'll look at the time the moon is rising,' Boris took a small diary from his pocket and flicked through the pages. 'Okay, there is newish moon around that time but it doesn't rise until early morning, and the sunset is around 21:50 so we'll go in at 23:00 it'll be really dark at that time.'

'Okay, I'll let Diedre know what you're considering. Should you change your plans, call me and I'll do the relay. I'll ensure a couple of our marines are nearby with a 4x4 and I'll let you have their mobile number as soon as I get back.'

'Yeah, and don't forget to remind Diedre that the spot she's chosen is to be completely clear of trees and no overhead wires.'

Carrie nodded. 'Right, now I'll take you down to the chopper company and you can check in with them. As far as insurance is concerned, that's covered, the United States will stand as surety and I've confirmed that in writing, so all they'll want from you is a copy of your licence.'

'Don't worry about taking me down there, I'll find their offices, it's better that you get back and control things from the embassy.'

Carrie agreed, and told Boris where the office of the helicopter company was. 'Oh, and by the way, I've brought you some detailed maps of the area and marked the coordinates Diedre gave me, you'll be able to work out from there where you can land to wait until you're ready to move.'

Boris thanked her and she left.

'Boris looked at his watch, it was 15:00 hours and still Wednesday 27th May, it had already been a long day. He walked back to the car and told Mikhail what the arrangement was. They drove over to the commercial section of the airport and quickly found the company called Horizon Jets who were situated on the airport periphery not far from the main building.

Mikhail parked the car in front of their small office block and Boris walked in to the reception area where a middle-aged woman in uniform met him.

'My name is Boris...'

'Ah yes sir,' she answered in Russian, 'we've been waiting for you to arrive. We've just had a confirmation the Bell Jet Ranger will be returning here about 18:00 hours, we'll need to check it out and refuel it, so I reckon you can take it at around 19:00 hours, will that be okay with you?'

Boris nodded, 'is that time pretty certain, as I've to pick my passengers up from Eisiskes near the border with Belarus,' he lied, 'and I'd like to do that before nightfall.'

'Oh, that's no problem,' the receptionist said, 'It will only take you about twenty minutes from here. Now sir if I could just have your licence so I can take a copy of it, the American Embassy has made all the other arrangements. If you'd like to turn up here by say 18:30, you can take the aircraft as soon as it's refuelled.' Boris thanked the woman and went back to the car telling Mikhail what time they should return.

'I think we should go back to the car park at the airport, study the maps of the area and then have forty winks in the car. Neither of us have had much sleep, and flying a helicopter when one is overtired is not the safest way to go, even if the Jet ranger is a pretty simple aircraft to fly.'

Mikhail agreed.

Boris had just nodded off when his phone rang.

'Hi Boris, sounds as though I woke you up,' said Carrie, guided by the muffled sound Boris made.

'Yeah, we were just catching some R&R, as we've been on the go since early this morning. What's the news?'

'Okay, I've the mobile number of the senior marine, there'll be two of them and they'll be armed.'

'What sort of armament?'

'Sub-machine guns.'

Boris grunted.

'Do you require them to carry something heavier?'

Boris thought for a moment, 'no but they could bring a couple of spares just in case, we had to leave ours with Diedre and George in case we got searched at the border point.'

'Okay, and I'll give you the marine Sergeant's mobile number, you got a pen?'

Boris scrambled about in the glove box looking for a piece of paper. He then realised he could simply put it in his mobile.

'Got it.'

'Anything else?' asked Carrie, 'Oh I forgot, I asked Diedre about the ground you're to land on and she told me George was trained on helicopters as well as F16's, so he knew precisely what sort of ground you'd need.'

'Okay Carrie, many thanks, you won't hear from us now unless we have a problem, so we'll be in touch tomorrow, oh yeah, one other thing, where are we all sleeping tonight?'

'Good thinking Boris, the two of you are booked in to The Campanile Hotel it's near the airport and Diedre and George are booked into a hotel out of town.

'I'll give you coordinates as soon as I have them, it's a small hotel in its own grounds south of Vilnius and just west of the E85 it's called Country House Prie Merkio. I'm arranging for the chopper to land there but I've yet to receive confirmation from the owners that they'll put lights on for you. Again, I've stressed that the landing ground must be level and free from any sort of obstructions, or overhead wires. It's essential that neither George nor Diedre are seen until we've completed our plan for them and this hotel is the last place on earth that they would be expected to stay.'

'What if they can't accommodate the chopper landing?' asked Boris.

'In that case, the Marines will drive them there.' Just as she finished speaking her mobile rang.

'Carrie...'

'Okay thank you.' She picked up the external phone to Boris, 'That was the embassy receptionist with the coordinates of the hotel and confirmation regarding the chopper.' She gave the details to Boris.

Within seconds of the call Boris was asleep; he woke again at 18:00 hours when his mobile alarm went off.

He decided to go up to the airport building to freshen up and he returned in time to drive the car to the helicopter company. He and Mikhail parked and locked the car, as they walked into the office the same receptionist greeted them.

'Oh hello,' she said, 'I've good news for you the Jet Ranger was returned early, so it's ready for you, I'll just introduce you to our senior Captain who will satisfy himself that you're comfortable with the aircraft and then you can go,' she smiled.

Boris walked around the aircraft with the Captain who confirmed that he was happy; he signed a form proffered to him and climbed into the left-hand seat, after noticing the call sign LY-OBD on the side of the helicopter. Mikhail went to the right side. Boris moved all the controls, the rudder pedals that controlled the rear rotor, the stick that came up through the floor that controlled the cyclic pitch and finally the lever that resembled a large hand brake on a car that controlled the collective pitch and on the end of this was the twist grip that controlled the throttle.

As the engine was a jet the throttle controlled the engine revs automatically, unlike a piston-operated helicopter where the pilot controlled the twist grip. He twisted the grip as far right as it would go and pressed the starter button on the console in front of him. The jet engine started immediately and the rotor circled above him gaining speed.

Boris put on his earphones and signalled to Mikhail to do the same. He pressed the intercom button to ensure they could speak to each other, then he switched on the radio and turned the dials to the correct frequency.

The rotors were now spinning at their maximum speed, so Boris called the tower, 'this is Jet Ranger helicopter Oscar Bravo Delta asking for clearance to take off travelling south east at 1,000 feet, 2 souls on board.'

'Oscar Bravo Delta, you're clear to take off at 160 keep clear of the light aircraft.' Boris knew that light aircraft parked on the ground could, in certain circumstances, be overturned by the wash of the helicopter rotors.

'Roger to that,' he replied as he moved the aircraft forward on the air cushion that had been created by the downdraught. Once clear of the light aircraft Boris lifted the lever thus increasing the overall pitch of the rotor blades but maintaining the cyclic pitch through the joystick so the machine was travelling faster but at the same height, about seven metres from the ground.

Boris explained to Mikhail who asked why they didn't take off straight up, 'helicopters can of course take off vertically, but there's a general rule that if there is room for a forward take-off that's the option taken by helicopter pilots. The reason for this,' explained Boris, 'is that if the machine suffers an engine failure at less than fifty feet, there's no time for auto rotation to enable it to land safely.

'So, it's a matter of speed plus height that's crucial for an aircraft to come safely down without an engine. The gap is called a "dead man's curve", which is why the spectator will notice that most pilots will stay close to the ground until a certain speed is achieved, before gaining height.'

Once lift was achieved, the helicopter soared into the air and a slight movement of the joystick adjusted the height as the control tower called him.

'Oscar Bravo Delta, please turn onto decimal 410 to connect to air control.'

Boris moved from his present radio frequency that was ground control to air control.

'This is Jet ranger Oscar Bravo Delta we're 160 at 1,000 feet towards Eisiskes, 2 souls on board.'

'Oscar Bravo Delta clear at 160 at 1,000 please be aware that you'll be travelling near the border and keep at least 1 kilometre west of that area, out.'

'Yeah,' said Mikhail, when the air controller had signed off, 'we wouldn't dream of going over the border would we Boris?'

'Of course not, at least not in the next hour,' he grinned.

They reached their destination in just under twenty minutes and Boris landed, while Mikhail got out and skirted the area. When he returned, he told Boris that there was a large clearing in the wood almost opposite where they planned to cross, and confirmed that the aircraft hidden from the border area would be the best place to fly from. Boris took off again and landed in the clearing shutting off the engine as he did so. Mikhail climbed back in to the cockpit and he looked at his watch. It was just before 20:00, another three hours to wait.

About an hour later, the two marines who had driven down from Vilnius approached them and introduced themselves.

'Where are you guys crossing?' asked one. Boris answered, 'almost directly east from this point, we shouldn't take longer than three to four minutes, assuming our "parcels" are still in one piece over there,' answered Boris.

'Can you check before you run?'

'You bet,' answered Mikhail, 'we'll make contact a few minutes before.'

'Okay,' said the marine, 'when we hear you starting up, we'll position ourselves close to the wire,' he pointed in the direction of the border fence, 'and if you run into trouble, we'll try and give you support.'

'Great,' answered Boris, 'just make sure that if there's any shooting, it's not in our direction, these aircraft aren't armoured.'

'Yeah, we'll see if we can miss you,' said the second marine grinning. 'Oh, and Carrie asked us to give you these,' he handed over two sub-machine guns, before returning to their vehicle.

Boris reckoned that it was the longest three hours he had spent for a long time, but he spent part of it checking the sub-machine guns, to make sure everything worked okay. they did.

THE HIDE

Chapter 19

Diedre and George were spending an uncomfortable evening in the 4x4, particularly so as it had been raining quite heavily earlier in the evening. They awoke to find the windows steamed up but because of their concern with the noise of an engine running they couldn't start the motor to demist them. It was also very cold and they had no blankets on board, so George had climbed out of the car in order to walk around and get warm. He heard voices nearby, and what sounded like a group of people walking towards them. He immediately crouched in the wet bushes and peered through them into the blackness. The voices came nearer and he recognised the language as spoken by a Russian not a person from Belarus. His heart pounded as the voices came even nearer, he reckoned that they could only be a few feet away. He'd left his gun in the car and he hoped to God that Diedre didn't wake and open a car door, as to do so would almost certainly give them away.

George was hugely relieved when the voices passed and gradually faded going south of their position. He knew from their conversation that they were part of the Russian contingent, and he guessed they were patrolling the area.

He crept back to the car and shook Diedre awake telling her what had happened.

They agreed then that both should keep a watch on the area, until about five minutes before the time of the chopper landing. They'd buried the Stinger and the missiles plus one of the sub-machine guns earlier in the day, which left them with one automatic and two machine-guns. George was conscious that he would be carrying the package in his new case as well and at the last moment he decided to bury his machine-gun gun as he wouldn't have enough free hands to use it anyway. The automatic he shoved into his waistband. While waiting, he had a thought and took one of the new shirts that he'd acquired in Kiev; he methodically wiped all the surfaces inside the car, taking care to include the steering wheel. Just in case, he thought to himself.

He'd heard the Jet Ranger's engine earlier and knew that Boris was waiting for them the other side of the border. Diedre's mobile rang.

'Parcels in place?'

'Go, go, go,' answered Diedre. Immediately afterwards they heard the jet engine start again, George waited until he could hear it in the sky. He then pulled the pin on one of the grenades and tossed it into the car. Diedre had shown him how to alter the fuse from five seconds to five minutes, but as there were a further five grenades on the back seat, he didn't want either of them to be in the vicinity when it blew. They both rushed out to the pick-up point and George flashed the light he'd taken from the car and gave the agreed signal.

The Jet Ranger almost landed on top of them, George opened the rear door and pushed Diedre in with his case. Mikhail had moved to the back of the cockpit before take-off to give cover from the north side, his sub-machine gun poked through the window.

George shut the rear door and climbed into the right front seat as Boris turned the helicopter and started moving towards the border fence. He'd reached about 300 feet when George felt the aircraft shudder. Boris let out a yelp and blood started to spill on to the centre of the cockpit, at the same time George could feel the aircraft starting to spin. He knew immediately that the aircraft was hit in the rear rotor and as Boris's right arm appeared to be incapacitated, he reacted fast and slammed down the lever on his left to take off the pitch. He knew that to auto rotate down with a lost engine was relatively simple, but the loss of a rear rotor was quite another thing as it was necessary to glide down immediately and land much the same as a fixed wing aircraft, not easy in a confined space.

There was however nothing Boris could do as the rudder pedals were of no use, and his right arm that was holding the joystick was also useless. George yelled as he snatched the stick from Boris, 'I have command. I've got the stick and will try to bring her down.' George was right handed, so this compounded the problem, but amazingly he managed to land, albeit not too smoothly on a patch of grass a few hundred metres clear of the border fence. It was then they heard a large explosion, and George assumed it was the car they'd left behind.

'OUT, out,' yelled George, 'and run for the trees,' which were only about 100 metres away, he switched off the engine and ran after the rest of them, as soon as they reached cover George had a look at Boris's arm with the help of the flash light held by Diedre. Mikhail stood behind them to shield the light from the enemy. Something, probably a piece of shrapnel had gone through the fleshy part of the upper right arm but it didn't appear that the arm was broken. George delved into his case again, took out a second new shirt, and tore it into strips using it as a bandage.

It appeared to work fine and then George returned to the helicopter to assess the damage. He realised that it couldn't be flown back, but it was important that it be removed as soon as possible from the present site, so he went back into the wood, and asked Diedre for her phone. She held her hand up, 'it's okay, I'll do it,' she said. It was only then he was aware of what sounded like a fierce gunfight going on over the border.

'I guess it's our marines,' said Mikhail, 'they said they'd give us cover, but I think they have taken our safety to heart.' Shortly after the two marines were seen running towards the clearing, 'got at least five of the buggers,' said one, 'but what was the explosion?' George told him. 'Well that was useful because it was getting a bit hot out there, and that made them disengage, I guess they thought they'd been out flanked,' he said grinning.

'Okay,' said George, 'we've one wounded and although it's not serious, we have to get Boris to hospital, have you guys a car that's large enough to take all of us?' asked George.

The Marines laughed, 'yeah, we came down in an armoured humvee, just in case, so we'll all get in fine, by the way I'm Sergeant Tucker, and this guy is private first-class Sean Haughty. We're part of the US Services team sent out under NATO to bolster the Lithuanian army, we only arrived a few days ago, and we were given temporary embassy duties.'

As the party started to climb into the humvee, Diedre took out her phone and having ascertained a number from Boris she punched it in.

'Carrie.'

'Hi Carrie this is Diedre, sorry to call you at home.'

'Oh Diedre, I assume all went to plan?'

'Not quite, we were shot at while flying over the border fence and a lucky strike hit our rear rotor. To cut a long story short, we managed to land okay, but the chopper is disabled and it needs to be moved before daylight, can you organise?'

'I'll get on to the US services team immediately, they have got some heavy lifting kit so shouldn't be a problem.'

'Okay, second problem, Boris was wounded, it's not life threatening, but he needs a hospital, can you suggest...'

'Yes, is Sergeant Tucker there?'

'Affirmative.'

'Okay, tell him to take Boris to the US military hospital at their camp near Vilnius, I'll alert them. What sort of wound is it?'

Diedre told her.

'Right, I'll call you back when I've everything organised.' Carrie cut the connection.

Diedre climbed in the humvee, and once all the doors were closed Sean Haughty, who was driving, slammed it into reverse and then forward. George found the seats so uncomfortable that he sat on his case, much to the merriment of the rest of them. It was Sergeant Tucker who remembered that there was a comprehensive first aid kit on board, and he re-dressed Boris's wound with a proper dressing.

Their first stop was at the hotel where George and Diedre were booked. They left their sub-machine gun with Sergeant Tucker and took only their overnight bags, one of them with the package containing the secret papers.

When signing the register, they explained that the helicopter they were flying had developed a mechanical problem, so they'd hitched a lift from an army vehicle. With the restaurant closed because it was very late, they managed to get some sandwiches made before turning in.

Had there been an outside observer, they would have been surprised to note that George and Diedre went in to the same bedroom.

Carrie phoned Diedre just as she was climbing into bed to let her know that she had arranged for the helicopter removal before sunrise and that Boris was being well looked after in the military hospital.

THE BETRAYALS

Chapter 20

The next morning, Thursday 28th May George and Diedre rose early, Diedre went into her own bedroom and ruffled the sheets to give the impression that she'd slept there and she showered and dressed in the bathroom.

At breakfast, they discussed the day ahead. 'George you have to call the Russian Embassy here, but obviously you'll need to do that from a call box in Vilnius so that they can't trace the call.'

'Yes, after that I'll put the package in a deposit box at the bank with the papers, and about three hours before the plane is due to take off, I'll collect my passport and tickets from the airport and check in.'

'Okay, I'll hire a car from Hertz and collect you from the airport after you've checked in and you can make a further call to the Russian Embassy from there.'

'Good,' said George, 'I think we've got everything under control, so if you'll organise the car, we'll start the day.'

Before the car arrived, George transferred all his belongings, apart from the documents from his case, into Diedre's.

'At least I'll have something to change into tomorrow,' he said.

The car was delivered at 09:00 hours enabling George to drive Diedre to the American Embassy and drop her off there to deal with other matters including the helicopter removal, checking that Boris was okay and organising the plan they had agreed for later in the day. She went to talk to Carrie who was acting head of station while her boss was on leave.

'We're sorry about the chopper and hope it didn't cause you any embarrassment,' said Diedre.

Carrie laughed, 'not at all,' she said, 'you see we actually own the helicopter company.'

Diedre looked surprised. Carrie explained, 'it was probably before your time, but the CIA owned a small aircraft company called St. Lucia Airways, it was a good little airline that ran between the various Caribbean islands in the 80's.'

'Why on earth...?'

'Ah, you see if you have a national airline,' explained Carrie, 'then you have a right to an International slot at a major airport, and the one we chose was Brussels where we ran C130's to Angola.'

'Oh, running arms...' said Diedre.

'Yes, exactly, until one day they landed in Angola and the crew were overwhelmed and murdered by the opposition. As a result, it became public knowledge and so the whole outfit closed except that it owned a couple of Helicopter companies that weren't involved. We still have them,' she smiled.

'That explains why you were able to get the aircraft moved and repaired so quickly,' said Diedre.

George arrived at the bank at 10:00 hours and asked to see the manager giving his name as Rolandas Giedrimas. It was an appointment that had been set up the day before by Jim Wallace using an alias. He was not kept waiting and was shown immediately into the manager's office and offered a seat in a comfortable chair. The manager appeared shortly afterwards.

He introduced himself, opening the conversation. 'I have been informed by your secretary in Ukraine that you want to open an account with us, and I've prepared the paperwork for you to sign. As you're a citizen of Lithuania, I've no problem in welcoming you as a new customer to our bank,' he smiled.

'Thank you,' said George pulling the file towards him and signing the individual forms as required. He used a CIA safe house as his address. 'I'll be transferring €100,000 as soon as I've confirmation that the account is live, I also want to organise a private safe deposit box...'

'Ah, yes, your secretary mentioned that fact, and I've asked the deputy manager to come up to meet you, he'll accompany you down to our vaults, I assume you have something that you want to leave today?'

'I do,' answered George.

As he finished signing the various documents, there was a knock on the door.

'Come in, ah Mr. Bartkus, this is Mr. Giedrimas, a valued new customer to our bank, he wishes to open a safe deposit box account and I would like you to take him down to the vaults and explain the procedures.' He turned to George, 'because we haven't received any transfer into your new account, I'm afraid I'll have to ask you to pay cash for the first month of the safe deposit box, after that the charge will be automatically deducted from your account.'

'Of course,' said George, 'I've a debit card, you can take US$5,000 from that to deposit into my new account and then you can take the safe deposit charge for the first month's rental.' He handed over the card, and received a receipt for the amount drawn. The manager thanked him profusely for his business and asked for his passport, which a secretary took a copy of. With that finalised, George shook the manager's hand and left the office following Mr. Bartkus. They went to an elevator and once inside, Bartkus pressed minus 1. The door opened and after a short walk they arrived at the safe deposit box section.

'I am not sure what size box you require Mr. Giedrimas...?'

George showed him the case he was carrying and said that he would like to deposit the whole case into a box.

'Ah, then we'll need to take a large box and that'll cost...'

'Oh, don't worry about the cost,' said George, 'as long as the contents are safe.'

Mr. Bartkus assured him that they would be completely safe.

'Tell me Mr. Bartkus, what happens if I want someone else to open the box on my behalf?'

'Ah, that is not a problem, providing the person has a key to open the box and can provide the password that you'll put on the form I'm about to give you.'

'Fine,' said George, 'it may well be that I'll authorise others to open the box from time to time.'

Mr. Bartkus nodded. 'That's accepted, we keep a different key here which has to be used as well as your key, so someone with your key and the password would have access.'

George put the case into the box provided, and slotted the metal drawer into the bank of boxes on the wall locking it with the key he'd been given. Mr. Bartkus then double locked the box and George filled in the form provided which gave the bank permission to deduct the cost of renting the box from his account, he put a password into the area provided on the form. The password he chose was NEMTSOV.

All the details completed, George shook the hand of Mr. Bartkus, and after being taken up to the ground floor, he left the bank heading for a public phone box, which happened to be only a few streets away.

He dialled the number of the Russian Embassy in Vilnius. A receptionist answered the phone. 'Good morning, may I speak to the person in charge of your political section please,' George said politely.

'Do you have a name of that person?' asked the telephone operator politely.

'No, but I've an urgent message for Colonel Sherepov of the FSB in Moscow. I'm in a hurry,' stressed George, 'my name is George Manning.'

The operator immediately recognised Sherepov's name and connected George to the commercial secretary, often the title given to FSB operatives in Russian Embassies.

'Good morning Mr. Manning, we've been expecting you.'

'Good morning, I'm calling to leave a message for Mr. Sherepov. I assume you're taping this information, so I'll make it brief. I'm in possession of something Mr. Sherepov would like. Tell him it's available for one million US dollars.'

'We need to have a meeting Mr. Manning so...'

'No meeting, the package he wants is in a safe deposit box at a bank in Vilnius, I'll send you the key and password when the money is deposited in my bank in the Cayman Islands, here is the account number.' George gave it to him. 'I'll call you again this afternoon at 16:00, if you don't have an answer for me, I'll offer it to someone else.' He put the phone down.

George then met Diedre at a pre-arranged spot and she drove him to the airport. George's plane was not leaving until 18:30, so they had lunch and Diedre told him that the helicopter been removed before sunrise, and was repaired by 10:00 hours before it was due to go out again. A piece from one of the rear rotor blades had gone through the rear window slicing into Boris's right arm. It appeared they were lucky, it could have been much worse. 'If you hadn't been trained to fly helicopters, I guess we'd have had a rather more difficult landing. Anyway, Boris is fine, he'd eighteen stitches, but he too was lucky it wasn't worse.' said Diedre.

The commercial secretary, who'd been talking to George, called in his assistant. 'Did you trace the call?' he asked.

'Yes sir, it was from a call box on the south end of King Mindaugas Bridge, he'll be well gone from there by now.'

'Okay, get me Colonel Sherepov on the line.'

The phone rang some minutes later.

'Sherepov.'

'Ah good morning sir, I hope you have fully recovered from your recent "accident" in Ukraine?'

'Thank you Vasnetsov, yes I'm almost fully recovered apart from my damned leg, anyway enough about me, do have some news?'

'Yes sir, I've just had a call from George Manning, he tells me that he has put the package you require into a safe deposit box in a bank in the city. He wants one million dollars for it.'

'Have you arranged a meeting with him?'

'No sir, he refused a meeting saying that I should pass the request directly to you, and that he would call me at 16:00 today to get confirmation, otherwise he will deal with the other side, he has given me his bank details in the Cayman Islands.'

'Hmm, clever Mr. Manning have you been in touch with our police friends in Vilnius?'

'Not yet sir, I thought I should report to you first.'

'You were quite right, but you should now contact the Deputy Chief, who we pay well for cooperation, he should be able to find out which bank George Manning deals with, oh and by the way, he may have registered as Rolandas Giedrimas, the name he used when travelling through Belarus. There is one other thing that is concerning me.'

'Yes sir,' answered Vasnetsov.

'I've a report here that there was an incursion last night by what appeared to be a private helicopter, the report says it was shot down, and crashed on the Lithuanian side, have you heard anything from your end?'

'No sir and I certainly would have done...'

'There's more, a vehicle was blown up in a wood which may have been the vehicle Manning was travelling in, I'll give you the coordinates so you can do some checking. The concern I have is George Manning may have been in a position to see things he shouldn't see do you understand?'

'I do indeed sir, but if he'd seen anything, I wonder why he didn't mention it when he called, such information may have been quite valuable.'

'Yes, but it may be that he's holding that for yet another day and more funds. The quicker you find this man the better Vasnetsov and the quicker he is dealt with the more comfortable I'll be.'

Vasnetsov nodded, 'I agree, leave the matter to me I'll get on to it straight away, what do you want me to say to Manning when he calls at 16:00?'

'Say I agree to his terms, but it will take a couple of days to arrange the transfer; he should call back on my number and you're authorised to give it to him.'

'It seems to me,' said Vasnetsov, 'that he's already burned his bridges with his own people, so the product he has for sale is worthless to him, who else would he sell it to?'

'I'm afraid we cannot take that chance Vasnetsov, the data he has is so sensitive that it could completely compromise our future plans, it is therefore essential that he's made to believe that we'll pay, but in the meantime, we can try to find where he has left it.'

Sherepov put the phone down. 'I wonder what Manning is up to,' he thought to himself.

He was soon to find out.

Vasnetsov made a secure call to the Deputy Police chief Sherepov had referred to, he was a man who'd been on the Russian payroll for some years, and as he had a propensity for a life of luxury including attractive women, he'd dug himself into a dependency on receiving his monthly cash payments.

'It's Vasnetsov here Gregor, we've information that a George Manning or he may be using the name of Rolandas Giedrimas has left something of value to us in a safe deposit box in the city. Through your contacts can you...?

Gregor laughed, 'I've just this minute had a call from the manager of the bank in question, it's the one you use for money laundering, obviously Mr. Giedrimas didn't know that a respectable English bank would be suspect.'

'Ah, that is good news, Moscow will be delighted. Can you arrange to...'

'Yes, I believe so I'll need funds for the manager of course.' *No doubt for yourself too,* thought Vasnetsov, but refrained from saying it.

'Believe me my friend that will not be a problem.'

'Okay, I'll need to obtain a court order as the bank won't have the other key, so we'll have to drill out the lock, I'll get onto that immediately.'

'Good, and at the same time we would like to meet this Mr. Manning, could you get your people on to his whereabouts, he called us only half an hour ago from the call box near King Mindaugas Bridge.'

'Can I say what he is needed for?'

'He is wanted for murder.'

Vasnetsov put the phone down and called Sherepov giving him the news. Sherepov was extremely pleased and congratulated him on the speed in which he had reacted. 'Remember once we have the package, we need to deal with Mr. Manning,' stressed Sherepov before ending the call.

Vasnetsov looked at his watch it was just after 15:00 hours.

George Manning called at the airline desk at 15:00 and gave the necessary details for the stewardess to hand him a package left for him by the embassy. It included his passport and a single ticket to Washington DC. He then booked early onto to the flight confirming that he only had a small bag, which he would take with him into the cabin. A boarding card issued, George then phoned the Russian Embassy at around 16:25 and asked to speak to Vasnetsov. The connection being made immediately, George listened.

'Ah Mr. Manning, I am glad you phoned, I've spoken to Colonel Sherepov and he has agreed your terms. He tells me that it will take a couple of days to get the funds to you and if you would let me know where we can contact you, I'll call you when the funds have been sent.'

George said that he would know when the funds reached his bank, at which time he would post the key and password to the Russian Embassy in Vilnius.

'Just one thing Mr. Manning, how do we know whether you'll do that, you could just take the money and disappear?'

'And look over my shoulder for the rest of my life, no Vasnetsov, I know how you deal with people who've betrayed you, and I've no interest in doing so. I'll call you as soon as the money is in my bank.' He ended the call and as soon as he had done so, he met Diedre at the airport entrance and they walked to the hire car, got in and drove south.

It was at 17:30 that Vasnetsov got a call from the Deputy Chief of Police. 'I've the court order and the locksmith here. I'll be travelling to the bank shortly. I also know that your suspect is booked on to a flight that leaves for Washington DC at 18:30, do you want me to have him apprehended?'

Vasnetsov thought for a minute, he looked at his watch, 'no I'm going to make other arrangements for Mr. Manning. Once I've done that, I'll meet you at the bank at 18:00.' He ended the call and immediately picked up the phone again, calling the engineers department at the airport. He asked for the Chief Engineer.

'Kiedis, is that you?'

'It's Vasnetsov here, I've an urgent problem it concerns flight 2341 to Washington DC flying tonight at 18:30.'

'It's delayed comrade, it will not now be going until 19:25.'

'Ah, better still, I want you to add the parcel we gave to you some weeks ago addressed to the Russian Embassy in Washington DC. You understand?'

'Of course, what is the timing?'

Vasnetsov worked out in his head the approximate time the aircraft would be somewhere across the Atlantic Ocean, 'say 22:00 hours, that should do it.'

'And the money?'

'I'll transfer it first thing tomorrow to your bank in Luxembourg.'

With that organised, Vasnetsov ordered his driver to take him down town to the bank where he was to meet the Deputy Police Chief.

In the presence of the Bank Manager who'd stayed at the bank after closing time, they drilled the safe box lock and the draw opened. Vasnetsov eagerly reached for the package and quickly looked through the contents. 'Good, good it all appears to be here.' He dismissed the locksmith, and as soon as he'd gone, the Police Chief received a thick envelope. 'No doubt you'll distribute this as you see fit comrade, you can both be sure that the President of our country will reward you in other ways, once we have control again.'

Vasnetsov returned quickly to the embassy

and called Sherepov, who was delighted. 'Please place it in the diplomatic bag for delivery to me personally tomorrow,' he said. 'What about Manning?'

'I've taken extreme measures to deal with the situation, he's leaving on a flight to Washington this evening, tomorrow the world will hear that another aircraft has blown up over the Atlantic. We will put out that it was organised by Islamic Extremists,' said Vasnetsov. 'We've had to call in quite a number of favours over this matter, so I hope this will be the final one.'

Vasnetsov was travelling home in his chauffeur driven car when his mobile went off. It was Kiedis, the Chief Engineer. 'There's a problem, Manning hasn't shown up even though he had a boarding card and the aircraft has been given permission to taxi out to the runway.'

Vasnetsov closed his eyes. The phone he was using was not secure. He had no choice but to give Kiedis new instructions. 'For God's sake get that parcel back, make any excuse, say that you believe some important part hasn't been checked, anything, but get that...' he heard a click at the other end.

Kiedis called the tower and asked them to re call the aircraft. He explained that a small but crucial replacement part had not been fitted and that the plane should return to the airport so that the matter could be rectified. He realised that he would have to report the matter the next morning, but he took comfort in the fact that he had prevented a disaster for no good reason.

After the parcel had been retrieved Kiedis called Vasnetsov at home again on an unsecured line and told him that the package was back in his hands.

So, where was George Manning, Vasnetsov thought to himself, he was dreading calling Sherepov in the morning saying that George had escaped their tentacles once again. He need not have worried.

Diedre drove across the Polish border at around 19:00 hours and then headed for Warsaw, where she caught a plane for Washington DC the next day. George was not with her.

Reported in the newspapers the next day was an article stating that a body found by the side of the road about 30 kilometres south of the Lithuanian border belonged to a person who had been shot in the face four times. Searching his clothes, they found two passports, one in the name of Rolandas Giedrimas, and one in the name of George Manning.

The US Embassy in Warsaw was informed and they confirmed that it was George Manning, an American citizen. George's tearful wife flew out about a week later and although she couldn't recognize his face, she confirmed that it was obviously her husband as the body had a small tattoo on an unmentionable place. She explained that on the successful passing out of the top gun exercise, each pilot had been tattooed with a small eagle.

It quickly became public knowledge that an unknown assailant had shot George, probably a Russian hit man who'd committed the murder.

The information got to Sherepov before it reached Vasnetsov and when the latter called the next day, he received the news.

Vasnetsov frowned, 'but it wasn't us comrade, we missed him at the airport, he'd checked in for his flight, but was a no show which is why we had to call the plane back.'

Sherepov nodded, 'yes, it was almost certainly a CIA elimination, he'd a woman with him I believe, perhaps it was her, but no matter, he's dead and good riddance. This means that our sensitive information stays secret, just as important, we've saved one million dollars, we've got our secret files back, so we can continue with our plan "Operation Vilnius".'

Vasnetsov had a sudden thought, 'you don't think Manning's death was a put-up job to take us off the trail?'

'Hardly, he'd at least have waited for the cash, no Vasnetsov I think we can say that we've one less problem to deal with, and I congratulate you and your team for the work you've put in.'

Vasnetsov had a warm feeling when he put the phone down knowing that soon he would have considerably more authority and money. He was going somewhere, he thought.

Four days later, Monday 1st June Diedre reported to the special section in Langley, Virginia, where she worked and she put in a full report to her superiors including the demise of George Manning and a special section regarding the tanks they'd seen just across the border in Belarus.

Two weeks later Monday 15th June, after she'd delivered her report, she was surprised to be called back to Langley for a high-level meeting with her overall boss, who was Director of covert operations, his name was David Wise. She was ushered into his office and he told her they were due to travel to the State Department for an urgent meeting later that day. He also mentioned to her that the Secretary of State was to travel to Moscow in two days' time to meet with the President and Foreign Minister of Russia. The American Ambassador would also be present. 'I want you to accompany the Secretary of State.'

'Hang on David, I know the American Ambassador, and sure as hell she knows me.'

'Yeah, but not in the category you are going as, which will be as Senior assistant to the Secretary of State, we expect it to give her a shock which will create a feeling of panic, and when people panic, they act out of their comfort zone, which is what we want her to do. We both suspect that she's been shacking up with her Russian driver for almost two years, and that he was put in place in order to recruit her, which he's done with some success, but the day of reckoning has now come and it demands your special expertise.'

Diedre shrugged, 'is that it?'

'Not quite,' David Wise grinned. 'We have a problem, the DNA taken from the documents George Manning got do not marry up with the DNA supposedly belonging to the President that the Ambassador sent to us last year. We want you to obtain the correct DNA as without it the documents George took to Ukraine will not have the same authenticity.'

'And how do I...?'

'Oh, you'll think of something, I've every confidence in you.'

'Thanks David,' she said drily, 'Okay, I'll do it, but this is my last hooray, after this I'm quitting again and I'm going to settle down.'

David Wise nodded, 'Okay Diedre, let's talk about that when you return, even if you do decide to retire, you'll still be on our list, we sure would hate to lose your skills.'

On Tuesday 16th June Jim Wallace got off the phone to his counterpart in Vilnius and phoned Bill Cummings. 'Hi Bill, I've had an unusual request from Vilnius, have you got a moment?'

'Sure Jim, give me five minutes, I'll come down, get some coffee on.'

Bill walked into Jim Wallace's office some ten minutes later and sat down. The coffee served and the door closed, Jim Wallace spoke. You'll have heard the George Manning was killed?'

Bill frowned 'yes I do hope it wasn't us...'

'Well, I can tell you that it was and it wasn't when this is all over, I'll explain what I mean by that later.'

Bill nodded, 'okay Jim, what's the request?'

'When George and Diedre were hidden in the forest in Belarus awaiting rescue, they came across Russian tanks hidden under the trees, about one hundred of them, but because of their situation they couldn't look around further than the wood they were in, as they may have been spotted. The priority was to get the package out, which they did and the results from that have been spectacular, but again I'll explain all that later. The problem they have in Vilnius is that although there are American troops there, who were sent in recently to give them some comfort, there are no Special Forces.'

'If they need Special Forces why don't they simply fly them in?'

Jim bit his lip. 'Well, our guys are trained to go in with all guns blazing, and they are damned good at that. The Brit's however work based on stealth, they are past masters at reconnaissance over a period, this is just what we need in Lithuania or to be more exact, Belarus. We need to know just how many tanks are on that border, if it's mined, what the force is there for and most important of all, when it's going to be used. Do you think we could persuade Colonel Watson to look at the problem for us?'

'Hmm, we'll have to be careful Jim we don't want to suggest that our Special Forces are not as good as theirs.'

'Oh, they are not, they are just trained to do different jobs. Our boys' training doesn't include patience, they wanna get in there and sort the problem, their guys are better for this sort of job. In any case there are no special US forces currently available this side of the pond and I happen to know that the Brits are not able to carry out the full training they have been sent for, since more and more of the Ukrainian army are being drawn into the front line.'

Bill nodded, 'okay, I'll talk to Watson and see what he has to say.'

Later in the day Bill picked up the phone to Jim Wallace. 'Hi Jim I've had a word with Watson, and he in turn spoke to Captain Desmond who you'll remember was on the last exercise.'

'Yeah he and his boys did a sterling job for us.'

'They did, and what Desmond is suggesting is that he and Sergeant McCauley fly over to Lithuania to do a reconnaissance of the area along the border on the Lithuanian side. He wants to get a feel of the place and consider the number of men that would be needed. Watson suggested he could get his information from a Google map, but Desmond disagreed. He said they should go up there incognito so that no feathers are ruffled. Once he's been to the area, they'll return and make their recommendations.'

'Do they want to inform the Lithuanian government?'

'No, not at this stage, and from what you've told me, it's too leaky up there, better we keep the whole thing under wraps for the moment anyway.'

'I agree Bill, when could they be ready to go?'

'Tomorrow morning on the early flight, and Desmond reckons he only needs three days up there. Watson tells me there's no need to get permission from higher up, we'll have to inform the British Ambassador of course and get his approval. I'll call him now.'

'Okay, let's do it...'

Bill phoned back within the hour, 'I've spoken to James Winston-Jones and he said that it was Watson's decision and not really within his remit, but he thanked me for keeping him in the picture. He did say that should they be required to go up there as a team, then a higher authority would be required.'

'That's great Bill, I look forward to hearing Desmond's report when he returns.'

The next morning Wednesday 17th June, Captain Desmond and Sergeant McCauley boarded an early plane for Vilnius. On arrival they hired a car and drove to an area that Boris had told them he had crossed over in the helicopter. They'd been told an infra-red search had already been carried out by the US air force but it had come up with a negative report.

John realised that could indicate there were no troops yet in the area or the troops that were there were wearing special clothing to mask the heat given off by the human body.

The vehicle they'd hired was a 4x4 and they travelled over 160 kilometres along the border area. Stopped twice by patrols, John told them they were looking for rare birds and the patrols believed them because they were Englishmen.

Three days later, they returned to Ukraine and Desmond and McCauley arranged a meeting with Colonel Watson and Jim Wallace to give their report.

John opened the discussion. 'The first thing we noticed was that the border on the Lithuanian side is not mined, whereas the

Belarus side certainly is. The second thing was although we spent three days there, we only came across two Lithuanian patrols, there appears to be no static control centres, which would make any invasion a piece of cake.

'We didn't see any tanks, so they are obviously well hidden, nor did we notice any tank tracks, but most of the area around the forests has been ploughed for no apparent reason.

'We listened in for radio traffic which would be normal for a large force, but there was very little, so if there are guys there, they are under instructions to stay silent.

'If an invasion is being planned, then it's not in our view immediate, as they would have to lift a channel in their minefield before starting up. That wouldn't take long and could be done overnight, but that would mean them setting off at close to dawn, not the best time for a major incursion. They have two parallel steel fences about eight feet high, this would have to be removed to allow tanks to move across. Tanks and their crews require substantial support, not only infantry but logistics, medical and replacement ammunition. Boris tells me that George saw none of that support in the forest.

'Our conclusion is that the tanks have probably been placed there to sit and await a situation where they will be used. It's likely that there are tanks in situ in other areas, 100 tanks wouldn't be enough to invade a country that's supported by NATO. Again, it's my opinion it would take at least three months to get all the forces together to make an invasion feasible, but if they have armour both north and south of that position, which is highly likely, then they could form an effective pincer movement and take Vilnius within a few hours.'

Jim Wallace sat back in his chair. 'Hmm, that's most interesting Captain Desmond, particularly so as the pincer effect was mentioned in the documents we were given.'

John nodded, 'yes, and if they have similar assets on the Baltic side, they could overrun the whole of Lithuania quite quickly, then of course Latvia and Estonia would be at their mercy, as the Russians would have cut off the southern access.'

Colonel Watson interjected, 'but what about the NATO air force, if they were brought in quickly, the armour would be neutralised.'

'That depends on how quickly these guys move, if it's a complete surprise attack, by the time the planes were in the air, the tanks would be in Vilnius, and NATO couldn't afford the collateral damage that would come from that.'

'So, they would take Vilnius, and seal the southern border within hours, I can see that,' said Colonel Watson.

'Yes,' said Kieran, 'and don't forget the southern NATO border is only with Poland, and that is barely 100 kilometres long. Not much of a border to hold with a well-trained army, don't forget also that the Russians have excellent air capability, so it would be a piece of cake for the Russians to respond to any belated NATO force.'

'Okay,' said Jim Wallace, 'do you have a suggestion?'

'There's only one,' answered John.

'And that is?'

'You can't afford to be caught by surprise, if NATO are in a position to catch the tanks as they are crossing the border from Belarus, you could really fuck up their plans and give time for an operational response both with ground forces and air.'

'So, we need some surveillance on the other side?'

'Yes,' said John, 'and the best way to do that to cover the three wooded areas, i.e. centre, north and south, is to build three tunnels underneath the border fence from a wooded area on the Lithuanian side to the wooded area on the Belarus side.

'Obviously, we need to ensure that each contain military assets, but it wouldn't take long to organise that, given reasonable warning.

'The tunnels need to be about 1,000 metres plus on each side of the border making a total length of each tunnel over a kilometre, you would also have to construct the tunnels on the Belarus side with a "dogleg" to ensure safety for the participants.'

I don't follow,' said Jim Wallace frowning.

'Well if our guys are discovered, you don't want a situation where grenades are rolled down into the tunnel, you've got to have a safety section they can hide behind.

'Anyway, that's a detail, but the problem I see is if as you say the government is "leaky" then anything like building tunnels would soon be compromised.'

'Hmm,' Jim Wallace looked at Colonel Watson. 'I think it's important to put you in the picture here,' he raised his eyebrows.

'I agree,' said the Colonel.

'Right, we sent George Manning through Belarus with the package brought back from eastern Ukraine. We'd two reasons for doing so, we wanted to be sure that Manning wasn't implicated in Mary Clancy's murder and the information he had brought out of Russia was not faked by the FSB, it was a highly unlikely scenario, but we needed to be sure.

'Assuming George was on the level, we guessed that the FSB would soon realise he'd escaped the explosion and had brought the documents to us here. Once the "bandits" knew they were in our possession they wouldn't have the same value, so after we'd determined the DNA taken from the signed assassination orders and made exact copies of them, we persuaded George to take the original documents by road through Belarus to Vilnius. The plan was to give the impression that George had turned traitor and had escaped via Belarus to Lithuania where he was to offer to sell the documents back to the Russians.

'The plan worked better than we thought, we were able to confirm that a senior banker of a British bank in Vilnius was in cahoots with the Ruskies. We'd previously suspected that his branch was money laundering for them and now we know that the guy is working for the other side. As soon as George opened a safe deposit account there, the banker contacted a Deputy Chief of Police who helped them retrieve the documents without them paying anything for them. We advised George to demand one million dollars for the documents, the money to be paid into a

Cayman Island account, which we set up. We discovered the Deputy Chief of Police had discussed the matter with a highly placed and trusted aide to the Lithuanian President, so that was a bonus, catching two in the net at the same time.

'When you read the action document George brought out of Russia, one can imagine just how easily an assassination of the Lithuanian President could be organized, as her trusted advisor has knowledge of all her movements. Finally, we found out that the Chief engineer of Vilnius International Airport was prepared to put a bomb on a flight that George was supposed to be on. We picked up these calls that were not made on open lines, thanks to your guys in GCHQ.

'Fortunately, the package was removed when George didn't show, but we had plans to halt the aircraft taking off at the last minute. We also have the names of two policemen in Belarus who took a bribe, possibly useless at this stage but could be useful if either of them climbs the promotion ladder.'

'What happened to George Manning?' queried John.

Jim Wallace sighed, 'he was unfortunately killed while driving through Poland, almost certainly the FSB caught up with him.'

'But I suppose convenient from your point of view, particularly if they suspected George had seen the tanks,' said Kieran, proving his cynical nature.

Jim Wallace showed his displeasure at such a suggestion with a frown.

'Okay,' said John, 'if you accept our recommendations, how do we dig tunnels without alerting the Lithuanians?'

'I've an idea,' said Kieran. Everyone turned to look at him in surprise.

'We already know there are no control areas along the border in Lithuania, only border posts at entrance points. It would be possible for NATO to follow up on our assessment and recommend three fortified border posts in the position we suggest.

'If the Russians were made aware about these hidden in the woods, it wouldn't in any way divert them from their plans, indeed they may consider that such a suggestion would give comfort to the Lithuanian government. Ostensibly these posts will be built to hold say six border guards and it could be stated they were there to catch smugglers. Once built, we could then surreptitiously dig the tunnels by using US forces trucks to move the earth at night. No one would guess we were burrowing underneath the border.'

'That's a very interesting idea McCauley,' said Jim Wallace, 'I'll talk to our engineering department to see how that could be done without arousing suspicion. Now let's assume we can pull this off, how would you use the tunnels?' He looked at John.

'We would have our own people in each of the three units who would take it in turns to watch the area. We would disguise the opening on the other side, so it wouldn't be found. By this method we'd have a good three weeks or more to assess an imminent attack and alert you guys so you'd have time to prepare a suitable response.'

'So, you'd recommend 18 special forces people in total?' asked Jim Wallace.

'Correct, but we wouldn't have to take all the positions up until we discovered movement in the centre section, then we could expand the number of observers very quickly.'

Colonel Watson cut in. 'obviously, we're going to need high-level permission for this, but if approved, I recommend that the number of people who are told about the tunnels are restricted to very few. My people would also want to know who would pay for this, and who we could we get to make the tunnels, as clearly we couldn't use Lithuanians.'

'Yeah, good point Colonel, I guess there may be some miners around the Wilkes Barre area in Pennsylvania who we could contract out to, there's heavy unemployment in that area now, so possibly we could find guys who'd been in the forces before becoming miners. We'd need to keep the whole thing under wraps, not easy, but not impossible either. Okay gentlemen, I'm going to discuss this with my people, Colonel Watson, I'll leave you to deal with your side, and I suggest we meet here one week from today to make some decisions. Finally, I'd just like to thank Captain Desmond and Sergeant McCauley for the work they have put in so far.' With that the meeting broke up.

Diedre'S REVENGE

Chapter 21

Monday 22nd June

The Secretary of State climbed on board Air Force 2 along with his retinue for the visit to Moscow. The plan was that after his meetings in Moscow he would then fly to the Middle East to deal with the worsening situation with Iran and Israel. Those not concerned with the second part of the trip were to be flown back to the States direct from Moscow in another aircraft. Diedre was on the latter list but it had been arranged that her aircraft would stop off in Vilnius where she had been asked to call in to see the American Ambassador. All people on the mission slept on Air Force 2 from Washington so that on arrival in Moscow on Tuesday 23rd June, they were ready to go.

The principle reason for the Secretary of State meeting the Russian President was over the indicated threat by the Russians that they would have used their nuclear capability to ensure the annexation of Crimea, if the West tried to interfere.

At the request of the Americans, the meeting was arranged with the minimum amount of people so the Russians had decided to use a small room off the President's office with a round table and seats for only eight people. On the Russian side there was the President, the Prime Minister, Foreign Minister, and a senior secretary. For the American side there was the Secretary of State, his Assistant, the American Ambassador to Moscow and Diedre.

The Secretary of State had a private prior meeting with the American Ambassador, so it was not until the party congregated in the Kremlin that the American Ambassador noticed Diedre. She could not believe her eyes and she immediately approached her. 'What on earth are you doing here?' she asked.

Diedre smiled without answering, just as the Secretary of State saw both women together, he went across. 'Ah Ambassador, you may not have met Diedre Robinson.'

'Diedre Robinson,' she repeated with a quick intake of breath, 'yes we've met but under very different circumstances, I'd no idea...'

They then went into the meeting, but the Ambassador's face had turned pale.

The President and Secretary of State, seated opposite each other at a large round table, the rest seated next in accordance to the country represented. The usual pleasantries were dealt with and coffee was served. Water glasses placed on the table with a jug of water and when the door finally closed, the

President raised his eyebrows. 'You asked for this special meeting Secretary?' It was a question rather than a statement.

'Yes, Mr. President, we were concerned about your threat to use nuclear weapons if things had not gone your way over the Crimea incident.'

The President remained impassive.

'I asked for this private meeting with you to avoid any embarrassment to your government at what I've to say. My President wants you to know that we have a complete understanding of your nuclear capability both on the ground, and those weapons connected to your air force and submarines. You will recall that President Reagan started an overall defence system of the United States, a project that eventually brought the old USSR to its knees, as you couldn't afford to keep up with the expenditure that was required for you to accomplish the same protection for your country.

'We've moved on from those days, and we are aware of your increased expenditure on your military including the improvement of your nuclear force.

'My President wishes to warn you that should you decide to use nuclear force, we have it within our power to negate your nuclear weapons before they leave your land space, which would mean that your land, large as it is, would be showered with nuclear fallout. We can destroy Russian submarines with their own weapons, the same goes for your aircraft. Those ships that are carrying nuclear weapons are identified, and in instances where you're using foreign bases such as Syria and Cyprus, the local governments will be made aware of the dangers to their own population in the case of war.'

The Prime Minister was now looking extremely uncomfortable although the President remained impassive.

'That deals with the nuclear aspect, now I've a final message for you personally. If you continue to grab or annex parts of sovereign territory belonging to other countries, you'll create a situation where we will be put in a position of no choice. We'll be forced to act...'

The president held his hand up. 'Mr. Secretary, I've taken note of your threats. NATO is weak you cannot even persuade your members to pay the required amount from their defence budgets to ensure an adequate response. There are certain areas in Europe that belonged to Russia, we fought hard for such a buffer and we bore the deaths of over twenty millions of our population securing our borders. Due to the weakness of our economy in days gone past, we gave all these territories back, and you have taken advantage of this by placing your weapons on our doorstep. You can be sure that we will not take back what is not ours,' he lied, 'but we will secure our borders from your creeping influence. You criticise us for aggressive tendencies, but you ignore what you did in Iraq and Afghanistan, and the interference in many other countries in the world. You should understand that your world power is waning, it's Russia and China that have the strength of purpose to succeed and we shall do so. If NATO attacks us, you can be sure we'll respond in kind, we'll then see how the economically weak western powers manage. We recognise that you're still a major threat to us, but I repeat, your partners are weak not only militarily but also financially, take the Euro, deliberately weakened by the Germans to help the German economy. Because of the value of the Euro, the Germans have been able to excel with their exports at the expense of the rest of the European partners. These diverse interests mean that you cannot even agree to work together peacefully, what you would do in war is frankly laughable. Europe is our domain you would be wise to look after your assets in the Pacific.'

'And you Mr. President,' said the Secretary of State, 'would be wise to look after your back door, which the Chinese have coveted for the last few hundred years. Consider what a European war would do to Russia, the Chinese would be quite happy during such a conflagration, and at the end of the day, you should fear China, not Europe or the United States.'

The President smiled, 'our strength is that we fear no one, Mr. Secretary. You must understand that democracy is a failure, because of the greed of your people. At the end of the day, you must fail.'

The Secretary of State stood up, 'Mr. Hitler thought the same, bear in mind what happened to him.'

'Hitler was a fool he had the world in his grasp, and threw it away. We'll not make the same mistake. Good day Mr. Secretary.'

The President got up and without shaking hands, walked out of the room followed by his Prime Minister and senior secretary. The

Foreign Secretary stayed and although now standing went up to the Secretary of State with a friendly smile. 'I am not sure what you feel you've achieved by this meeting,' he said, 'our President is not the sort of man one can threaten...'

The Secretary of State laughed, 'you're certainly correct there. If I were Russian I would no doubt end up in a coffin by the end of the day.'

The Foreign Minister smiled, 'if you were Russian, you wouldn't be so stupid as to make your...'

There was a splintering of glass on the tiled floor. Everyone looked round to where the noise came from. Diedre was picking up the shards of glass from the glass of water the President had been drinking from.

'I do apologise,' she said, looking somewhat crestfallen, 'I was walking round the table and my folder caught the glass of water...'

'Please leave the glass,' said the Foreign Secretary, 'the cleaners will deal with it.'

Diedre nodded and dropped the pieces she'd picked up.

Later when she was alone with the Secretary of State, he asked her if she'd managed to get what she came for.

Diedre smiled, 'Yes, I'd an identical glass in my bag and it had some water in it, we knew of course the type of glass used by the Kremlin, so when I dropped it, I was able to use the diversion to put the President's glass in my bag.

'There is no doubt that the American Ambassador suspected what I was doing, so I

235

expect some problems before returning to the plane.'

'Hmm, in that case you'll fly with me Diedre; I'll get the pilot to divert to Vilnius before going to the Middle East. I'll phone the pilot now so that he can change the flight plan, it'll only add a couple of hours to my schedule, but that's no problem.'

'Yeah, that would be helpful,' said Diedre, 'it's obviously imperative that I get this glass back to the States, and the easiest way to do that is to put it into the diplomatic bag going from Vilnius.'

'I assume it's already in a suitable container?'

Diedre nodded. 'It's in a sterile container, what time do you intend to fly?'

'I think if you have completed all your other business,' he looked at Diedre.

'Yes, the quicker we move out the better.'

'In that case, I'll just say cheerio to the Foreign Minister, and we'll go straight to the airport.' On the way out of the Kremlin, they said goodbye to Emilie Dixon the American Ambassador who by then was standing by her chauffeur driven car talking to a Kremlin official. She gave Diedre an odd look. 'Are you staying on a few days?' she asked.

Diedre smiled, 'I'll have to see what the Secretary of State requires me to do,' she answered.

'Well I hope you'll drop in and see me if you have the time.'

Diedre just continued to smile.

Air Force 2 took off for Vilnius as planned. When Diedre dropped off in Vilnius later that afternoon, she heard the latest news from the

American Ambassador to Lithuania who met her at the airport, he told her of the death of the American Ambassador to Moscow in a car accident. He had no more details than that, but hoped that when they got back to the embassy, more information would be available.

When they reached the embassy, Diedre handed him the glass that was now encased in the sterile sealed bag, and said to him that it was essential that it be included in the diplomatic bag leaving that evening. He called in his assistant and gave him instructions to do just that.

'Now,' said Diedre, 'what's the problem?'

'It's delicate,' he said, 'we've found out that a senior aide to the President is working with the Russians. Now we know that the President is very anti-Russian, but she relies on him completely which means that we have to be extremely careful what she is told.'

'How did you...'

'Find out?'

'Yes,' answered Diedre innocently.

'It was thanks to a man called George Manning who crossed over the Belarus border recently with some important papers that had been taken from the FSB files.'

Diedre smiled, 'yes I'm aware of that.'

'Unfortunately, he was killed, shot by an assailant, believed to be a Russian hit man in Poland as he was heading towards Amsterdam to fly back to Washington.'

'Yes, I'm aware of that too.'

'Okay, while George was in Vilnius, our people, with the help and support of GCHQ in the United Kingdom, picked up some phone calls that compromised a Bank Manager, a Deputy Police Chief, and a senior aircraft engineer working out of Vilnius airport. They also caught a call between the Police Chief and this aide, which left no doubt as to his affiliations. The problem is that this man went to university with the President, she won't hear a word said against him although we have tried to make her see reason.'

'So, what do you...?'

'I'm afraid there's only one answer, Diedre, we need him taken out. But of course, there is no way it can be attributed to us.'

Diedre nodded, 'okay tell me some more about the man, what his habits are, what sort of car he drives, where he lives and so on.'

'I'll give you his file,' he handed over a thick folder. 'I can provide you with a secure office so that you can study his details.'

'Okay Ambassador, leave it with me for an hour, and perhaps we can meet again, after that and I'll tell you what I need.'

The Ambassador called in his assistant, 'Marcus, show Ms Robinson into the secure meeting room. Did you get that package away in the diplomatic bag?'

'Yes sir.'

Diedre followed the young man and he showed her into the meeting room that was very similar to meeting rooms in all American Embassies, a large long table with 12 leather covered chairs and a couple of telephones on a small table in the corner. She noticed the TV screen on the wall. She wondered to herself whether the security officers in the embassy were aware that smart televisions could now be hacked and both audio and visual recordings made from outside the building. She made a note to talk to her people when she returned to Washington.

Marcus had left telling her that he would be just down the corridor and she should call him when finished.

Diedre read the file quite quickly and was ready to see the Ambassador after only forty-five minutes.

When back in his office, she remarked, 'It appears that he owns his own single engine Cessna aircraft,' she looked up from the folder in front of her.

'Yes, I believe so,' he said, 'in fact he is quite an accomplished pilot, and flies to his Dacha every weekend.'

'Good, what I need is the following.' She handed over a list to the Ambassador. He frowned, 'I'm not sure what this is?'

'Three critical parts on the running of the aircraft, each part has a code for diagnostic purposes, I need those codes. It's a matter of National Security, so Cessna, being an American company will be able to supply them. They will also know if they have supplied any upgrades so you'll not need to look at the actual aircraft. I'll speak to your political guy here and instruct him what to do once he has these codes.'

There was a knock at the door, and the young assistant walked in to the Ambassador's office with a piece of paper.

'Ah, this may interest you Diedre. It's a report on the accident in Moscow.'

Diedre raised her eyebrows.

'The initial report states that the chauffeur was driving the Ambassador back to the embassy, when inexplicably the throttle stuck at full open. The driver tried to stop the car with the brakes, but they failed too. He then pulled the handbrake on, but by then the car was doing over ninety on a free-way within Moscow. The car slid sideways and then turned over rolling several times. Apparently, the Ambassador never wore the rear seat belts. The impact threw her out of one of the rear doors, which became detached. She died at the scene, but the driver survived probably because he wore his seat belt.'

'Oh dear,' said Diedre, 'we do seem to be losing people quite quickly.'

Before she left, she spent half an hour with the technical man connected to the CIA in Lithuania and gave him specific instructions.

THE WAITING GAME

Chapter 22

Diedre returned the next day to Washington DC and thence to Langley leaving her report along with a note for David Wise, that she didn't wish to be further involved with the CIA, she then left the building without meeting him for what she considered was the last time.

Captain Desmond and Sergeant McCauley returned to Jim Wallace's office a week later than originally arranged on Wednesday 1st July. Present at the meeting were the usual faces, Bill Cummings, James Winston-Jones and Colonel Watson.

'I believe Colonel Watson has some news for us,' smiled Jim Wallace.

'Thank you, Jim,' said Colonel Watson. 'We read Captain Desmond's excellent report on the reconnaissance he and Sergeant McCauley carried out and we've agreement in principle from the Lithuanian authorities to build three fortified border posts close to the border with Belarus.

'These units are to be constructed in thick concrete and to be impervious from small arms fire or even RPG's. They'll be designed to hold up to six soldiers who will live inside the units.'

'Thank you, Colonel Watson,' said Jim Wallace, 'from our side, we have permission from our top brass to build three secret tunnels from underneath these units with a length of 1,000 metres or more depending upon our needs. The size of the tunnel is to be 3 metres in width and three metres high. We'd have liked it to be larger to allow vehicles to be driven through, but this request was denied on both cost and the fact that a much larger tunnel would be much more difficult to disguise and would arguably take too long to construct, therefore the tunnels will only be accessed by troops. Concrete steps will lead the way down to thirty metres underground. This should mask the sound of the drills, in the tunnels.

'The tunnels near the end on the Belarus side will be dog legged as recommended by Captain Desmond for about twenty metres and the steps built up to the surface to be covered with a hydraulic trap door which will be camouflaged with foliage. CCTV cameras hidden in trees at the other side will ensure checks be made before emerging from the tunnel, these to be placed by Captain Desmond's men. Telephone wires fixed for the length of the tunnel will ensure proper communications and the switchboard will be in the centre unit allowing secure conversation between all the three units, each unit attached to a phone near the opening on the Belarus side. There will be no ring tone, just a flashing red light. The centre unit connected to the main telephone exchange so that it will act as the control unit for all three.

'We are however prepared to be flexible as the contractor may have other suggestions once he has seen the plans.

'Finally, we've decided to install automatic flare units along the whole length of the area between the three units that will be controlled from the centre unit. This means that in the event of a night time invasion, the flares can be activated from the central point, giving brilliant light to the whole area.'

'That's impressive,' said John, 'but how long is this going to take?'

'We are assured by the US contractor who will oversee the whole project, that subject to a site inspection, he will finish the whole job within three months. We'll use Lithuanian labour for the fortified units. For the tunnels, we aim to ship in specialists from the States. The Marines will police the area to stop any interested parties looking. The Lithuanian authorities have said that they'll construct razor wire along the whole area behind the units, to create a "dead ground area".'

'And who is paying for all this?' asked Colonel Watson.

'Uncle Sam,' answered Jim Wallace, 'it's in fact being allocated out of the CIA budget, but we consider this so important that we even went to the President to be sure that we were well covered politically.

'Now Captain Desmond and Sergeant McCauley will temporarily be attached to the marine division and they will monitor the building of the units, reporting back to me and Colonel Watson if any extra help is needed. You will also have to have hand-picked the guys who are going to man the units once finished.'

John Desmond nodded, 'that's not a problem,' he said.

'There is one more bit of sad news I've to impart to you, in fact two bits of bad news. The American Ambassador was killed in a car crash in Moscow, the same day that the US Secretary of State was meeting with the Russian President. We think that this was organised by the Russians.

'I also have a report that the senior Aide to the Lithuanian President was also killed last weekend when flying his plane back to his home. That appears to be due to an engine problem in the Cessna 172, but an investigation is still being carried out.'

Kieran frowned, 'that sounds to be rather convenient, doesn't it?'

Jim Wallace grinned, 'not for us to reason why, God moves in mysterious ways.'

'Yeah, doesn't he just,' Kieran scowled.

'Okay gentlemen, if there are no more questions, I will leave it to you guys to get yourselves organized and we'll arrange for you to be flown up to Vilnius. Oh, I forgot to mention we're recommending that you live on the site, so portacabins will be set up for that purpose.'

John Desmond who was aware of the planning machinations that preclude people from building homes in Britain was amazed at the speed of the acceptance of the Lithuanian authorities and he found there were already workmen on the site when he arrived there. These first workers were not aware of the tunnelling project. The outside of the units were finished in a record time of just over four weeks and the interior a further two weeks. John took over the finished product at the end of just six weeks, 20th August Thursday, the same day the President of Lithuania, gave a carefully selected public the opportunity of inspecting the work, after she formally opened them.

Kieran noticed that the president was still wearing a black armband over her dress.

All this was of course before the tunnelling started. The day after the official opening, Friday 21st August the work started in earnest by specialist contractors flown in from the States. The excuse given was that the final work had to be completed and only specialist workers could do that, which was of course true. They were told they had six weeks to complete and so they worked in shifts, the surplus earth being taken away to fill an old quarry, which was to become a housing estate, some few miles away. Nobody bothered to question that.

The three areas closed to the public were guarded by American marines, which meant that only those with special passes could gain entrance to the site.

The senior contractor soon realised that the specifications for the tunnels had to be altered, he pointed out that the depth had to be substantially deeper and he suggested that they go down to 50 metres, similar to the depth of the Palestinian tunnels dug under the border with Israel. He indicated that such a tunnel would be very difficult to detect while at the same time the depth would cover any noise made by the digging machinery. He also pointed out that the length of the tunnels would have to be well over 1,000 metres to ensure the entrances at the other side were well out of the way of any troop movements in Belarus. The last point he made was the width. 'If it's your intention to eventually send troops in to out flank the enemy you'll need to widen the tunnels to around ten metres.'

'How much longer will all these changes take?' John asked. The contractor told him that it wasn't a case of time, rather the cost. 'It would also help if we embedded steel ladders at the opening and closing entrances so that we could dig straight down and straight up at the other end. This would allow us to restrict the noise that would be created at the Belarus end by having to create steps.'

It all made good sense and John immediately contacted Jim Wallace with an indication of the difference in cost, which was substantial.

Jim came back within 24 hours, and said they would agree the extra cost, but would deduct 5% for every week that the contractors overran.

'We reckon that this project will save hundreds or perhaps even thousands of lives and help to halt the incursion policy of Russia for some time, cost is not the major factor here, the successful completion is,' said Jim Wallace.

John said afterwards to McCauley that the beauty of working with the Americans was once committed they got things done, 'I wish we could do the same sometimes,' he said wistfully.

John also spoke to the contractor and told him the terms, which were agreed to. He said he would contact his head office to ask them to obtain a new contract from Langley. The signed confirmation came back, within a few days and work started immediately.

Two days before the deadline on 21st September the tunnels were finished; an extraordinary feat of cooperation, good logistics, sweat and hard work. John sent Kieran to inspect the other two tunnels and he concentrated on the centre. A seamless sliding door in one of the internal walls hid the steel steps from the centre of the above ground unit. This led to a small room where the end had three steel ladders like those seen in fire stations, that the fireman can slide down quickly. As he walked along the tunnel, he noticed a covering on three sides of rust proof steel sheeting that met the concrete floor. There was a shaft going along the right side at the top of the tunnel that had openings every 5 metres in order to draw out foul air and pump in fresh from the Lithuanian side. The air cleaned by a unit in the room from where the tunnel started. Lighting was subdued.

John noticed that there were CCTV cameras pointing towards Belarus every 100 metres, monitored from the same room that contained the air-cleansing machine. These had been set high up in trees on the Belarus side by his men. They worked by wireless to ensure security. Every 250 metres there was a small cupboard set into the wall with wires stretching back to the unit. Desmond knew that if compromised the high explosives contained in them would destroy the tunnel. After 1,000 metres, it seemed the tunnel ended, but on reaching it, he realised that there was a passageway leading to the right for about ten metres and then the left again. Once he reached 1,200 metres, he came to a wall with similar ladders to the one at the beginning of the tunnel.

He climbed up to near the top and turned on a small monitor which was attached to six cameras set in various places in trees, giving a complete view of the surrounding area.

He was aware of these, as again his own men had been responsible for setting them up to avoid detection. These video links were replicated in the room next to the unit. By the monitor was a button that activated the hydraulics to open the door placed in the forest floor. After checking the monitor, he pressed the button, which noiselessly opened the large trap door.

He noted that if he took his finger off the button it stopped immediately. There was a second button, which allowed the closing of the door, but he also carried with him a remote control that had the same action to be able to operate the door from outside the tunnel.

Once the door was open, he climbed through, leaving the contractor behind. When he closed the door with his remote, he found that it had a very bushy tree attached to the roof, which completely disguised the entrance.

He also found a well concealed "hide" that had been built nearby by his own soldiers which gave excellent camouflage for up to three persons. After having a quick look around, he opened the door, and climbed back into the tunnel, as he was sliding down, he pressed the remote and was pleased to see it close seamlessly on top of him.

'Excellent,' he said to the contractor waiting at the bottom, 'I expect you'll want to get your men home ASAP, I am certainly happy to sign off on this one, and if McCauley's report is good, then you can all go home.' Desmond smiled.

The contractor shook his head, 'you're correct that we can send most of our guys back,' he said. 'But I'm going to leave two of my people in each unit in case of unforeseen problems, if after a month everything is okay you can send three of 'em back, but we'll keep one guy in each unit until whatever it is you are doing, has been accomplished, this is a direct instruction from Langley.'

John nodded, 'yeah that's sensible, but remember you guys aren't soldiers, so there's no way you can go out of the other end of the tunnel.'

'Don't worry, we'll be very happy to stay the right side of it, but we'll be available if anything goes wrong.'

Jim Wallace had been watching the reports on the construction work going on in Lithuania, and was delighted when John sent him an encrypted message through the American Embassy in Lithuania that the work had been completed and he was about to start the surveillance in earnest.

Wallace told Bill Cummings and it was arranged that they would meet with Winston-Jones and Colonel Watson as a matter of courtesy. In fact, both had received the news through other channels. During the meeting Jim Wallace said, 'my real reason for calling you together, is to let you know that the DNA Diedre Robinson captured from the glass from which the President of Russia had drunk, was positive, so that finally indicates that the DNA sample sent by the deceased American Ambassador was false, as we suspected. Of course, we had other conclusive evidence without that as we now have an asset within the Kremlin that confirmed her complicity.

'You'll shortly hear through your own diplomatic channels that we are jointly, i.e. the British and the US starting to build a case to put to the United Nations. We have the original DNA from the forms we received, we've the report that was supposedly put to the Politburo and the Russian assessment of their future aims.'

'But surely, the Russian's will simply claim them as fakes,' said Colonel Watson.

'Yes, of course,' answered Jim Wallace, 'so we need some more pertinent proof that they are following through on their secret aims and we're hoping to get just that from the Lithuanian situation.'

'One thing I'm puzzled by is why the American Ambassador to Moscow had to be "removed", surely it would have been better to leave her in place and feed her incorrect or incomplete material?' Colonel Watson proffered the question.

'Absolutely right Colonel, but since we received George Manning's report, we ensured she only received data that would not be useful to the Russians. She was no fool though and she must have known that things were not going her way. Once we'd made an assessment that George Manning was very definitely working for us, she would have guessed her usefulness to the Russians was limited. She was infatuated with the Russian chauffeur and would like to have crossed over, but we recognised that once she'd done that, everything we'd fed her would have been suspect and we couldn't afford to let the Russians know that we knew that she was a traitor.'

'But as I understand it, you weren't sure whether it was her or George Manning who was the rogue,' said Winston-Jones.

'Actually, we were pretty sure that George was okay, we got him to "escape" through Belarus as we had a report that Sherepov realised that George hadn't been killed in Ukraine, so we had to suggest to them that he was only interested in money, not his country. It worked, although there were some difficulties on the way, but we made sure that by putting Diedre with him, and following up with Boris and Mikhail, we would be able to ensure his safety.'

'But you didn't, as in the end he was killed while driving through Poland.'

'Yes, but that wasn't our doing, still it didn't really change things, as the Russians believed that he was crooked, and as they managed to get hold of the package without paying him the money, it was imperative from the Russian point of view that he be "killed" in case he had seen the tanks hidden in Belarus. Of course, they were not aware that there was anyone accompanying him. 'If you think about it, as the Russians had no intention of paying him once they'd the documents back, they would have realised that George wouldn't have had too many alternatives. He wouldn't have had any funds to live on, certainly no pension from his employers, his only choice would have been to spill the beans...'

THE INVASION

Chapter 23

John Desmond got his men into place and they quickly discovered that there were almost 1,500 tanks on the Belarus border. They noted that there was increased activity in the area, as Desmond said, 'you can't leave sophisticated equipment in a damp environment without first class maintenance.' All movement by the Russians was made at night. Shortly after the Lithuanian tunnels were completed, special Russian living quarters started to appear under cover of the forest. One of Desmond's men inspected these units and it was realised that the quarters were protected against infra -red rays from the air, ensuring that human body heat was undetectable.

At first, the watchers couldn't understand how the logistics were working until they discovered tunnels on the Belarus side leading to large warehouses some miles away. Rail tracks laid within the tunnels for small electric trains took maintenance teams and spares to the collection areas within the forests. This also answered the question regarding wireless traffic being almost non-existent, as they had laid telephone cables between the warehouses and the tunnel heads. This of course suggested that the tunnels had been created some years before the incursion into the Crimea and Eastern Ukraine and were quite old. The question posed was how many other areas were under a similar threat. The State of Poland was particularly concerned at the news and as a result, was reinforcing its border positions.

Desmond had a difficult moment when the other side decided to scour the forests to ensure there were no watchers and he almost ran into a patrol using dogs to sniff out any potential hides. When the dogs approached where John was hiding, he knew that discovery was imminent, so he used a Dog Dazer, an electronic piece of equipment designed to confuse dogs.

He'd come across this in his early training and had bought one for his own use. The equipment, about the size of a mobile phone but thicker, when aimed at a dog at a range of about 10 metres, meant that the disorientated animal flees the scene. 'The beauty of this weapon,' said John, 'is that it makes no sound picked up by the human ear, but produces a very high frequency signal that disturbs a dog's equilibrium. It was quite amusing to see two large dogs fleeing the area with angry handlers following and shouting for them to return.' After that experience, John arranged for all the Special Forces on duty to have such equipment.

Over the following month there was much more activity as trucks were driven into the forest overnight along with armoured carriers, suggesting a sure sign of belligerent intent.

On Wednesday 14th October, John attended a special meeting of senior NATO members and he gave a report on the build-up of assets the other side of the Lithuanian border. The question asked was how and when an attack would go ahead and what excuse would be given, because the Russian population in Lithuania had experienced no unrest in the country. John reported that it was only when it was observed the insignia on the tanks and other vehicles were being painted over that the realisation of some action was imminent.

The American Aircraft carrier the George H.W. Bush had been on a visit to Portsmouth in England, prior to heading for the Mediterranean. However, due to Desmond's report, NATO decided that it should turn around and visit Gdansk in northern Poland in order to assure the Poles that the US was watching developments.

NATO in cooperation with the US and the UK had decided to play Russia at its own game and by the time the US carrier had reached Gdansk, 30 of their AV-Harriers were painted in Lithuanian colours but still flown by US marines, who had no insignia on their uniforms. They were flown to a strategic area in Lithuania near the eastern border, and kept in readiness, fully armed and under cover. An E-2 Hawkeye, a carrier based tactical airborne warning and control system, subsequently accompanied them. The same principles were adhered to with 30 Tornado GR4's flown out of Norway by UK pilots. This was also at the request of the Lithuanian government and it was to be termed a lend lease action for which NATO was not directly responsible.

The George Bush sailed north in the Baltic to visit Tallinn in Estonia before returning to the North Sea and it was planned that they should then sail to the Mediterranean, but they dallied on the way as they still had on board 30 F18 E/F Super Hornets available if the Russians interfered with their fighters.

It all started in western Lithuania where there were riots in Klaipeda, the third largest city in the country and one of the largest ports on the Baltic. The Russians complained of anti-Russian policies perpetrated by the local authority, after a Russian speaker from the region had attempted to assassinate the President. The city, which has a Russian ethnic presence of 28%, felt unsettled simply because one of their people appeared implicated in the plot, apparently hatched in Klaipeda.

The local security service suspected that professional activists were responsible for stirring up the fears of the Russian minority. There was also trouble in Visaginas in the north east where the Russian ethnic have a majority of 58%. Here someone unknown murdered a Russian boy of sixteen and a note pinned to his chest indicating it was an ethnically motivated atrocity.

It didn't take long for the Russians in Lithuania to become concerned for their safety, giving Russia the perfect excuse to invade on the pretext of safeguarding their kin. The Russian military reckoned they would take Vilnius within 12 to 24 hours and have the whole country under their control within 48 hours, long before NATO could react in force.

Klaipeda was only about 40 kilometres from the Russian Baltic State in the south and there were serious incidents at two of the major border crossings, one at Sovetsk and the other at Kybartei, resulting in Russian troops openly deploying at those two sectors. Not surprisingly, the Lithuanian army responded and cut off any proposed incursion into their territory. Unfortunately, this is precisely what the Russians wanted, and whilst the Lithuanian army was preoccupied in the west of the country, the Russians in the east were to make their move from Belarus.

John Desmond became aware of substantial movement on the eastern front and that mine clearance had been taking place in certain sectors during the night hours for the last few days.

He reported that soldiers, without insignia, on the Belarus side had marked out gaps of some ten metres with small green flags that would cater for about ten tanks, which meant roughly that there would be about 180 clear lanes available.

Engineers had placed explosives against the large fences that surrounded the border. Through knowledge gleaned from his special forces, he was able to pass on coordinates for each of those lanes. At about 22:00 hours on October 23rd to celebrate the onset of the Russian October revolution, they had finalised the mine clearing. Desmond knew that it would be unlikely that the units hidden in trees would move until around 03:00 the next morning, so he sent out a warning call to all units standing by on the western side including members of the Lithuanian army and US Marines.

These troops were placed in strategic areas, not massed in large numbers in one place, because they now knew exactly where the enemy was crossing the border and their commanders knew where to position the defenders. Even then, they were about half a kilometre behind the border to ensure protection from any air action.

Once the invasion started, the Special Forces planned to disrupt the rear-guard. To this end the Americans had released a thousand marines to filter through the tunnels as soon as the Russians moved.

To avoid detection before crossing the border the Russians had craftily kept their infantry in the warehouse area, to be deployed immediately the tanks crossed into Lithuania.

It was at 03:00 hours on 24th October, as John had expected, the tanks started up all along the line. Messages flashed back to the fortified units and they in turn contacted the various airfields where aircraft were waiting. It took 3 minutes to get them in the air and only five minutes for them to get to their allocated areas.

At 03:00 hours precisely, explosions were heard in the forests on the Belarusian side and gaps were blown in the fences. The Russian tanks started to move in single file through the gaps. Immediately the flares already hidden in the Lithuanian forest activated so the whole area was lit up as though it was daylight, and because they burned slowly, they created light for over an hour.

The Russian plan was that once their tanks were through, they would spread out into an attack mode, but as the third tank in each column reached a position where it would start to deploy, there were huge explosions created by the allied air ordinance. The leading tanks were immediately destroyed which meant that the ones behind couldn't move, some tried to get out of the column and take a route through the closed wire, but most who took that track were blown up by their own mines.

To create even more confusion the marines now appearing from the tunnels were blasting the tanks from behind thus trapping those in the centre. It was total chaos. The Special Forces, who already knew the opening areas of the enemy's tunnels, stuffed explosives into the electric trains, jammed the equivalent of an accelerator, and sent them back down towards the respective warehouses where they blew up by remote control creating huge fire conflagrations and trapping Russian troops awaiting transport to the border.

Some of the tanks managed to get through however, and they were met with Apache helicopters brought up from Germany a few days before and hidden at the edge of the forest near the fortified units. The tanks that managed to conceal themselves in the forest on the Lithuanian side were finished off with troops armed with Finnish LAHTI L39 20mm anti-tank rifles.

Within the first fifteen minutes of the incursion, one pilot reporting back to base remarked that the scene on the ground reminded him of the fleeing vehicles in Kuwait during the retreat of Saddam Hussein's army during the first Gulf war.

As soon as the aircraft dropped their smart guided bombs and missiles they returned to base, were re armed and took off again, the whole procedure taking only ten minutes.

The general in charge of the Russian army realised that the attack had been a disaster from the start, and called in air support from airfields nearby, he then sent the waiting troops up in the electric trains, and they were surprised to see what they thought were empty trains speeding in the other direction.

Waiting at the top of the tunnels were companies of marines who, when they heard the approach of the trains, fired missiles into the dark interior. Unlike the tunnels built on the Lithuanian side, the Belarusian tunnels were straight which meant that the missiles hit the electric trains heading towards the opening killing dozens of enemy troops.

Those enemy soldiers behind realising the tunnels were compromised, reversed their course only to find that there was no way they could get through due to the blowing up of the warehouse at the other end. Because smoke was starting to flood the tunnels soldiers rushed back and threw down their arms surrendering to the awaiting marines who took them and locked them into the blocks built by the Russians in the forest. One of these was turned into a first aid centre where wounded were being dealt with.

An early warning was given that enemy aircraft were heading towards the various areas and missile sites surreptitiously placed in hidden areas activated. At the same time fighter aircraft scrambled from the deck of the George Bush.

Two enemy aircraft shot down by missile sites near the border, blew up, after which the Russian aircraft withdrew.

The Russian General in charge now realised that the attack, which largely depended on complete surprise had been compromised. After speaking to his headquarters, he called the attack off. He told the tank commanders to return to their bases inside Belarus, those that could not get back with their tanks were ordered to leave them and walk back.

The whole business was over by 10:00 hours in the morning and the devastation caused was huge. The Russians lost over 800 tanks, two fighter aircraft and killed, wounded and taken prisoner exceeded 1,200 troops. Their tunnels had been destroyed as had the logistic warehouses and two Russian submarines had been sunk in the Baltic that had threatened the US task force.

There was panic in the Kremlin as scapegoats were sought for the failure and the propaganda machine was put into full steam. The story put out was that NATO had carried out a cowardly attack on Belarus forces, killing several soldiers, and destroying some infrastructure and that the President was now considering how to retaliate, including the use of nuclear weapons.

He quickly found however that his Generals were not in favour of such a drastic reply and it was made clear that such an order would be ignored. Was the first crack in the hierarchy appearing?

The Lithuanian government put out a press release that their country was subject to an invasion from forces behind the Belarus border, but without involving NATO they were able to repel those forces, which they claimed were Russian, with their own air force and ground troops. They hailed it as a similar defeat to that suffered by the Russians from the Finnish army in 1938.

While recriminations were going on in Moscow, the US and Britain were pulling in data gained for an emergency meeting which they had called for in the United Nations in New York.

THE UNITED NATIONS

Chapter 24

The meeting at the United Nations was set for Thursday November 5th. It was not lost on the British that this was also "Bonfire Night".

The Russians, supported by Belarus, laid a complaint about the incursion into Belarus territory of the Lithuanian army and air force. They also laid a claim that the US had put their large carrier into the Baltic in order to help Lithuania with aircraft and that they had deliberately sunk two Russian submarines that were peacefully patrolling International waters. Their case was that the Russian speaking population in Lithuania was being harassed. Russia could no longer stand by and allow the disgraceful attitude of the Lithuanians towards human rights. They also complained that Lithuania with the support of the Americans had moved troops into part of Russian territory that was situated on the Baltic Sea. China also supported the Russians in a belligerent speech that suggested they would be upping their military expenditure in support of the South China Sea and the disputed ownership of the islands therein.

The American Ambassador to United Nations then stood up.

'Mr. Secretary General, it's time that the world was aware of the danger to world peace represented by Russia. The Russian people are oblivious to the true facts, and our heartfelt sympathy goes out to those brave Russians who were either murdered or removed into the State jails for their belief in Democracy.

'I have here some documents, which I'll distribute copies to all members of the United Nations, they fall into three categories.

1. Assassination orders signed by the President of Russia,
1. A report supposedly sent to the Politburo in 2014 for which we have evidence that it was never circulated, and finally
2. A strategy document setting out Russian goals between 2015 to 2020.

'These documents came to us directly from a senior person working for the FSB, unfortunately she was brutally killed by the State, not an unusual situation in Russia if you disagree with those presently in power, as you'll see. Now it may interest the members that the first country on the list for destabilisation and incursion followed by invasion was Lithuania after which the sovereign states of both Latvia and Estonia were to be overrun.'

An angry murmur went up from the assembled body.

The Russian Ambassador stood up, 'These so-called documents are a complete fabrication and lies,' he stated.

The Secretary General intervened saying that the Ambassador would have his turn when the American Ambassador had finished his case.

The America Ambassador stood up again.

'Thank you, Secretary General. Now as to the validity of these documents, you should know that we have checked the DNA of the papers signed by the President and have found that they belong to only one man and that is the President of Russia.'

There was a temporary uproar when the Russian Ambassador interrupted again saying that the DNA details were obviously incorrect and faked by the Americans in order to destabilize the Russian State.

'Well gentlemen, the DNA taken from the papers was analysed by the Pharmaceutical laboratories of... he named a famous international company who were above repute, located in Switzerland; and this is the DNA data given by them.

'However, this meeting is about much more than that, it will be noticed that the report on future strategy mentions not only countries in Europe but also countries such as China, who they believe are future enemies. The Chinese are well capable of deciding how true this suggestion and the threat of incursion into their sovereignty is.' He noticed the Chinese Ambassador scowling at the Russian Ambassador.

'Now to return to what happened in Lithuania. I have here photographs taken during October of this year by infra-red cameras of some brave men who crossed the border into Belarus. Warned of an impending invasion plus the fact that Russian tanks placed under cover in woods next to the border indicated a belligerent attitude towards Lithuania. I've here some pictures you might like to consider.' Everyone looked at the large screen that had been set up in the conference centre.

'This picture is of a line of Russian tanks, you'll note the insignia on the back. Here is another picture of soldiers in Russian uniforms painting over the Russian insignias. Thirdly, here is that same Russian soldier some days later, with no insignia on his uniform, does that remind members of another situation in Crimea only a few months ago?

'Now, here is a picture of those soldiers clearing the minefield on the Belarus border and fixing explosive charges into the wire fences which surround the perimeter. Here is another picture of the tanks breaking through the border, just before the Lithuanian air force destroyed them.

'We now know that this incursion was planned at least a year ago if not longer, as tunnels had been built in order to facilitate the moving of ammunition and other logistics from warehouses a mile or so from the border, and here is a picture of one of those tunnels.

'Finally, those of you who represent the countries mentioned in the Russian strategy report should look carefully at your defence plans. The current President of Russia is intent on gaining territory that was lost in 1955, by destabilising parts of your countries that have Russian speaking inhabitants and then by encouraging more Russians to move into the area by offering attractive grants or / and free housing for properties stolen from the original indigenous people.

'They didn't achieve their objective in Lithuania because a very brave woman who worked for the FSB in their administrative office in Moscow, was so appalled at the murder of Boris Nemtsov that she handed these documents to our representatives there. As I've already said, she was almost immediately killed, but we managed with great difficulty to smuggle them out of the Russia.'

Before he'd finished, the delegates noticed that the Russians had left the centre.

THE POST MORTEM

Chapter 25

It was some weeks later that James Winston-Jones and Bill Cummings met over dinner.

'I just wanted to thank you and your people for the help you gave us regarding the Nemtsov affair, without Captain Desmond and his team we wouldn't have been in a position to do what we did.'

'Well it was very much in our interest to help, but I guess I still don't know the whole story,' answered James.

The wine waiter came with a bottle of fine vintage champagne that Bill had ordered and another took their orders for dinner. James decided to have the trout that was advertised as taking 30 minutes to prepare, which he said was fine as they had quite a lot to talk about.

'Well, you remember that it was Mary Clancy who was approached by Hanna Borsok who was the senior administrative officer within the FSB headquarters,' said Bill Cummins, 'she'd been a faithful servant to them for nearly twenty years, but she also happened to be Jewish. When a fellow Jew, Boris Nemtsov was killed because of his protest about the way Russia was being directed by the then Russian President, she rebelled, probably without fully considering the consequences.'

James nodded, 'she was either very brave or a little naive.'

'Well, whatever. What she didn't account for was her boss working on a Saturday, which meant that the missing files were discovered far earlier than she could have imagined. We know the result of that; Hanna was murdered. So was Mary Clancy, but Mary was smart, she'd already passed the files to George Manning. Of course, she'd no idea that they would be so desperate as to kill her, but she underestimated the fact that Emilie Dixon, the American Ambassador to Moscow was far more important to the FSB than she imagined.'

'Hmm, so George gained some time by heading for the war zone, which Sherepov hadn't considered.'

'That's right James, George was exactly the right man because he'd spent time in Ukraine prior to Moscow, so he'd friends there that supported him, but even then, because the fighting was hotting up, he couldn't risk trying to break out because of the original documents.'

'And that's where we entered the picture with our special services team.'

'Yes, and that was crucial, because we didn't know exactly where George was, although we'd a good idea, we had to be sure and Desmond and his team did a great job in finding him,' Bill laughed, 'although I'm not sure George appreciated his flight on the Apache.'

'Well, he was an ex-pilot, so he would have appreciated the need to get him out at speed.'

Bill nodded, 'yeah, but when he got to Kiev, we thought the destruction of the fortified farm where he was situated would indicate he and the documents had been destroyed.

'Sherepov was too thorough though and soon realised that George had got out, the problem we had then was (a), if they knew we had the documents they would lose their value to us, and they may well have changed their strategy so we wouldn't necessarily know where they were going to strike next. (b), they would be able to plan their response to any publication of the documents, and (c), they would have known that Emilie Dixon would be exposed, thus making any information we had passed through to her deliberately false, or of no value.

'So, we had to devise a way of making them feel more comfortable. We sent one of the documents with a diplomat to the pharmaceutical company in Switzerland who very quickly gave us the DNA from a sample taken from the paper, we knew then that the sample sent by Dixon earlier was false, but that still left the problem of us fooling Sherepov that we hadn't seen them. Diedre Robinson came up with the idea of suggesting George travel through Belarus as though he were looking to abscond with the documents to sell for a large sum of money. Those guys always believe that money buys everything in the west so Sherepov fell for that story, hook, line and sinker.

'To ensure that he be detected in Belarus, we let it be known, through a trusted contact of theirs, that George was headed there, but we didn't report the fact until we knew he'd crossed the border. We also sent Diedre with him and a follow up team of two Ukrainians who we'd recruited some years before, and who had proved their worth to us.'

'But you indicated to me that Diedre was there to check on George?'

'A white lie I'm afraid, you see we not only wanted George to get to Lithuania but we knew once he was there, he would "light" up some suspects. For instance, the Banker, who we suspected of helping the Russians launder money, the Deputy Police Chief, who was working with them. We guessed it was one of the deputies, but we didn't know which one and the senior aide to the President of Lithuania, which was a surprise although we'd suspected there was a top-level leak for some time, and finally the Chief Engineer at the International Airport, who we didn't know about either, but who compromised himself.'

James smiled, 'so you reckoned that the merchandise was so important to the Russians that they would risk almost anything to get them back?'

'Yes, that opened the door nicely, and enabled us to get George away.'

'But they caught up with George....'

Bill laughed, 'this is where the Poles were very helpful, they had a body in a mortuary nearby where the "incident" was perpetrated. They moved it to a site just off the main road and shot the dead guy in the face enough to ensure that whoever looked at him couldn't recognise him, and then we got a local tattooist to put on the symbol that George had on his backside. It was then announced that George's wife would fly out from Florida to identify the body which she duly did in a flood of tears, and that was that.'

'But what happened to Diedre Robinson?' asked James.

'After spending a few days in Poland, she drove George to Amsterdam, where they caught a plane to Washington. You see Diedre Robinson is Mrs. Manning, although I didn't know that at the time. She was working for SAD (Special Activities Department) a covert section of the CIA when she met George and it was, she who persuaded him to join the Agency. Diedre had retired from the service when they went to Moscow, but David Wise persuaded her to come back and carry out the job she did when George became involved. When she was in Langley she was asked to deal with the American Ambassador to Russia, you see Diedre had some very special skills, she was originally a very bright and talented electronics engineer before joining the service and it was she who invented the ability to hack into PCL's long before the technology was known by most.'

'What's a PCL?' asked James.

'A Programmable Logic Controller, a sort of minicomputer that runs most equipment nowadays, Diedre found that by using an electronic gadget which she designed, made it possible to control any modern car by a laptop computer nearby. You can imagine how useful this was to the agency, they no longer had to have hit men shoot people, they sent Diedre in to do the job. It was just a question of opening the throttle wide and keeping it open, disabling the braking system and interfering with steering, it's a far better way of getting rid of the ungodly than using nuclear polonium or such which is what the Russian's do.

'The only problem was that Diedre would only carry out these actions if she was satisfied that the person concerned was a threat to the State. Unfortunately, we loaned her to your guys in 1997. The security agency at the time persuaded her that the target concerned was a real threat to the British democratic system so she gave your MI6 the blue print for the electronic gadget she'd made. When she heard of the resultant killing, she was mortified, and resigned on the spot. The only reason she returned and accompanied the Secretary of State to Moscow was she'd an issue with Emilie Dixon, who'd done her best to kill her husband.'

James nodded, 'she also got the President's DNA which was different from the DNA Emilie had purportedly sent earlier to Washington.'

'Yes, they had a DNA machine with them in Air Force 2 which they took to the meeting, so they were able to get an immediate answer, once that was known, the new political man at the American Embassy in Moscow was advised by Diedre how to deal with her car using a laptop. She knew that the Russian chauffeur had recruited Emilie. He had cynically used her so Diedre had no compunction in what she did. She also knew that the American Ambassador always travelled in the back and didn't use a seat belt.

'On her way back, she gave the electronic apparatus to our Ambassador in Lithuania, they needed that because they were targeting an aircraft which would have been difficult to reach from a laptop. They in turn handed it to the Secret service there. They found a way to use it on a light aircraft, which dealt with the senior Aide. They arrested the Deputy Police Chief along with the Chief Engineer at the airport. Both are singing like you wouldn't believe, and they have been able to catch several others in the net. The bank manager concerned is now suspended and under investigation. All in all, an excellent piece of cooperation James, thank you,' he raised his glass just as the food arrived.

'One last question,' said James, 'what happened to George and Diedre?'

Bill laughed, 'I believe Diedre bought herself a large restaurant in the Caribbean and George stayed in Washington for a short time to help prepare the case for the United Nations, he is now heavy in computers also down in the Caribbean. He's cracking out some very accurate data culled from Cuba. In fact, we're still using him for certain sensitive work. But they make a good team, and we haven't seen the last of them.'

James frowned, 'Isn't it odd that Diedre would go into the restaurant business?'

'Well, as you know James, once in the security service, you're in it for life. Since you British pulled out in the seventies, the Caribbean has become a much more sensitive area for us as it's our southern flank and a great deal of our overseas oil comes up through the Windward and Leeward Islands.

'The island, where Diedre is, is a centre point, where better than a good restaurant near the sea to keep an eye on our interests in the area?

'But tell me, what about Captain Desmond and his team to whom we owe so much?' asked Bill.

'Ah, that could turn out to be an interesting story.'

Anything I should know about?' asked Bill, with a smile.

'Hmm, well let me tell you very confidentially, I assume you've heard the name Boko Haram?'...

The next day after the lunch, the newspapers were full of the newest story from Russia.

"It has recently been reported that the President of Russia has disappeared and it's rumoured that he has been removed from power by the military who are concerned about his wild threats of nuclear war and his aggressive plans regarding China.

"Because of his belligerent behaviour NATO members have at last woken up to the possibility of another European conflict and a few have increased their defence expenditures, or not reduced them as previously planned.

"The new regime in Russia is making friendly noises about an entente cordial with their European neighbours and it is hoped that they'll discuss the withdrawal of their forces from the Crimea and Ukraine in return for the ending of damaging sanctions."

After reading the story James telephoned Bill Cummings. 'You've read the story in today's papers I assume?'

'Yes, it appears we've seen the last of the Russian President, which must be good.'

James smiled, 'Don't believe a word of it Bill, 'The Bear' is still active as you'll soon see. We must be constantly on our guard. The planning of the Lithuanian affair was good, but it relied on it being kept totally secret. The next time they try something it will be much subtler.

The route taken by Diedre and George from the
Ukraine through Belarus to Lithuania

Printed in Poland
by Amazon Fulfillment
Poland Sp. z o.o., Wrocław

62482661R00157